To Emily

Sue Hzy x

In the strange world of ONGALONGING there are greedy volcanoes and flowers with big ideas. There's a dragon who once blew bubbles, and a broken-nosed fairy with a tool kit who's heading for the centre of the earth.

Not all the unicorns are white and not all the mobes remember who they are.

Deep in the bracken is a sour and growling metrognome whose head beats time, and the skies are bright with flutterpasts who live and die in one glorious day. And there to help them all is Oops the clumsy ongalong, sometimes drippy and often confused.

Full of colour, humour and riotous imagination, this is a fantasy that's closer to reality than it seems...

ONGALONGING

Like THE SNOWGRAN, Sue Hampton has learned that love is stronger than death. This, her ninth book for Pegasus, is for readers who like their fantasy to seem real as well as magical, and be deep as well as funny.

By the same author

Spirit And Fire (Nightingale Books) 2007
ISBN 9781903491584

Shutdown (Nightingale Books) 2007
ISBN 9781903491591

Voice Of The Aspen (Nightingale Books) 2007
ISBN 9781903491607

Just For One Day (Pegasus) 2008
ISBN 9781903490372

The Lincoln Imp (Pegasus) 2009
ISBN 9781903490389

The Waterhouse Girl (Pegasus) 2009
ISBN 9781903490426

Twinside Out (Pegasus) 2010
ISBN 9781903490457

Traces (Pegasus) 2010
ISBN 9781903490464

The Snowgran and Ongalonging

To Emily Slay, winner of Sue Hampton Mastermind 2010, and a talented young writer. Congratulations.

Sue Hampton

The Snowgran and Ongalonging

Pegasus

A CIP catalogue record for this title is
available from the British Library

ISBN-978 1903490 471

Pegasus is an imprint of
Pegasus Elliot MacKenzie Publishers Ltd.
www.pegasuspublishers.com

First Published in 2010

Pegasus
Sheraton House Castle Park
Cambridge CB3 0AX England

Printed & Bound in Great Britain

MEET MAYERLING

Mayerling was a long name for such a short dragon. His claws were as tiny as dewdrops. His rather stubby tail would not be much use for fighting (if he ever did any, which wasn't likely). And when he unfolded his neat little wings they only just spread out wide enough to keep him dry in a downpour. In fact, everything about Mayerling was small, except his deep, round nostrils, which were so dark that worms often got lost (and sometimes baked) in them.

There was no argument about it. Young Mayerling was the lightweight of the family. Sometimes his brother Kree liked to oink at the sight of him. Kree said Mayerling was so small he reminded him of a poor little piglet – the kind that has just been born and spends its time lying in straw, tugging at its mother for milk.

His brother Skraw didn't agree. He said Mayerling was more like a lamb, the kind that has difficulty standing up and bleats for its mother. "Baaa!" teased Skraw, and thumped his tail so high he nearly tripped over it.

Mayerling's brothers were bigger than he was. When the two of them were best friends rather than tail-thwacking enemies, they boasted that between them they could eat him for lunch – one bite each!

Mayerling was a long name for a very short dragon.

They called him Mayerling when they were being grown up and impatient, shouting for him because they were tired of waiting: "May..er..ling!"

They called him Mayerling when they were cross. They joined their dragon teeth together so that the flames had to squeeze through the gaps: "MAY..ER..LING!"

But when they were too sleepy or full or beautifully warm to remember how annoying he was, they called him Maya. And he didn't mind the name itself, not at all. The problem was the other words that rhymed with it. Sometimes, when they tickled him with tease-flames, Kree and Skraw used those rhymes to make his cheeks burn. Mayerling always told the truth. So his feelings were hurt when they said,

"Maya! Maya!

Such a little liar!"

He tried not to let his feelings show but sometimes, when he said, "I'm not! I'm not!" his round red eyes filled with stinging tears.

But of course the really obvious rhyme was the most important word in the whole universe for every dragon, large or small.

"A dragon called Maya just couldn't breathe fire!"

This wasn't true, but that wasn't the point. It meant he wasn't a proper dragon. It was rather like saying that a fish couldn't swim or a squirrel couldn't climb. Breathing fire was what made a dragon a dragon. Breathing other things, however interesting, just wouldn't be the same. But Maya had tried once, and his brothers had never let him forget how silly he looked.

"Maya's in trouble!

He only breathes bubbles."

That was almost true. Because when dragons reached their fifth birthday they had to test their courage by venturing out of their world and crossing into ours. It was a challenge and a long, dangerous journey. To prove they had been to the world of humans they had to return with evidence. Kree's flight home had been a struggle. The glob of melted can opener clutched in his right claw weighed him down at a dangerous tilt. And Skraw wobbled home with the stretchy pink of a plastic toy clinging to his scales like bubble gum. But most young dragons were less ambitious and simply brought back something scampery they'd crisped in a flame attack.

Not Maya. He carried bubbles in his nostrils, big, blue-tinged, soapy ones. But he didn't bring them back on purpose. He'd been flying past a human house when he smelt something flowery and followed his nostrils in through the open window. There he saw what he thought was a small pond that made a warm scented cloud. Nobody had told him about baby bath. Being different from other dragons, he had a wonderful splashabout before footsteps on the stairs scared him out of the window. Dripping and smelling rather lovely, he hurried back home.

Once they had stopped laughing at the soft floating spheres spilling up from Mayerling's nostrils, Kree and Skraw had asked for directions.

"Where there's baby bath," said Kree ...

"There's baby," said Skraw.

"YUM!" they said together.

But Mayerling never told them anything. He hadn't seen any baby, but if he had he wouldn't have said so. Because "Baby" was the other name his brothers used when they were fed up with him. So Maya thought that whatever babies were, and however juicy they might be, he was on their side.

The three dragons had a sister called Phue, but she was older than her brothers and thought they were so silly that she yawned whenever she heard them coming. Once Mayerling had been flying towards her so fast, and so out of control, that he had flown right inside her yawning jaws and nearly choked her. She had coughed him out again on a sea of flame and batted him away with a wing. His brothers were inspired by that:

"Mayerling's such a joker!

He's a little big sister choker!"

As for their dragon mum and dad, they lived busy lives. Hoski was a flying instructor. He ran advanced courses, for dragons who wanted to fly further faster, and in style. And Shika was the most famous dragon chef for miles. Her most popular takeaway dish was her spiciest chilli, thick with juicy slugs sliding through slimy sauce. It kept all her dragon customers happy and made sure their fire was always steaming.

The dragon parents loved their little dragons, but most of the time they let them amuse themselves. They trusted them to stay as safe as dragons can. Because dragons, being fire-eaters, fire-breathers, and fire-dancers, thrive on danger. It's what they love best.

But not all dragons are quite what you would call typical. Some break the dragon rules. They do their best to miss out on challenges, preferring naps in the sun. They don't like snake vindaloo whether the snakes are alive or dead, and they never fancy fried baby as a tasty treat, however peckish they are. These dragons have been known to land in awkward places, not because of their daring sense of adventure but because of their dodgy sense of direction. They don't hate cooling rain like other dragons, or fly away from it, screaming and hissing. In fact they close their eyes as the raindrops stroke their scales, and make a noise between "Prrr" and "Mmmm". So they enjoy the company of the ongalongs, or water squirters, that other dragons avoid and ridicule.

These dragons are rare. In fact, there's only one in this story, and I think you may have guessed his name.

Mayerling.

MAYA AND THE MEAN VOLCANO

Kree, Skraw, Phue and Mayerling lived with their mum and dad in a lively district famous for its volcanoes. Small but very fierce, they gathered in clusters and filled the air with red smoke shot through with flying rock. I mean that the volcanoes behaved this way, not the young dragons. But in the case of Kree and Skraw, who were even smaller and just as fierce, there was not much difference on a wild day.

The volcanoes were live, and that made them especially exciting. Not because they had legs and walked around erupting, but because they had stomachs deep inside their craters. They were always hungry for something hot and spicy to boil up and swallow. Sometimes the greedy volcanoes hurled out their leftovers into the smoke with the hot rock and lava. But anyone wanting to piece the bits together again (to reassemble a friend) might have trouble. Hoski and Shika told their little dragons not to take any chances. Because the live volcanoes lurked among the others trying to look as innocent as volcanoes can.

"Use your eyes!" said Hoski, pointing with a sharp claw to his own, which were scarlet in the middle and yellow as melting gold all around. "If you see the smallest tip of a curving tooth poking out of that lava, flap your wings and FLY!"

"Use your nostrils!" said Shika. "Sniff! If it's a live one it'll have very bad breath."

"Especially if it's eaten Maya for supper," said Skraw.

"No volcano would bother to eat Mayerling," said Kree. "Not even as a nibble between meals."

"Oh," yawned Phue. "Please go away! You're boring me to sleep."

Hoski and Shika wanted to be sure that their advice was understood. Volcanoes were fun. They gave dragons their own natural theme park, with deep down, sizzling dives and aerial obstacle courses. But they could be deadly. And the live volcanoes were sneaky. Sometimes they were so hungry they swallowed up regular volcanoes and took their place. And sometimes they gave birth to new ones that looked fizzy and harmless until some brave dragon flew too low above the steam, and disappeared with a flap and a crunch.

Mayerling thought there must be quieter places to live. Personally he rather liked the blue fields of soft grass where flowers tangled and kissed. He enjoyed the kind of pink and yellow skies that were not littered with hot, hissing rock. Now and then he longed for a swim in water that was not roaring and steaming but stroking white sand.

Kree and Skraw loved soaring and somersaulting around the craters, dodging the hot flying rock. **Mayerling thought volcanoes were trouble.** He'd rather not tease one, not even the doziest. He'd rather lie in the sun.

So when the little dragons got ready for a volcano day out, with curry cakes for packed lunch and flasks of chilli ginger to wash them down, Mayerling was in no rush.

"May..er..ling!" his brothers called, stamping their dragon feet and beating their dragon wings together.

"I've got tummy ache," groaned Mayerling.

"Too many spiced toads," said Kree, and made a hissing sort of laugh. Somehow Mayerling knew a rhyme was coming.

"Poor little Maya!

Not much of a flier!

The toads in his tummy

can LEAP a lot higher!"

Kree and Skraw did some leaping of their own. Maya didn't laugh. But he gave up pretending to be poorly and followed his brothers with a sulky pout of his dragon snout. He tried to keep up but soon fell behind.

Soon they were circling over the biggest cluster of volcanoes that steamed and bubbled and gurgled from deep down in their craters. Kree and Skraw looked excited. It was a battle and they were going to win it. No volcano was going to defeat or beat them. And there was no way a volcano was going to EAT them, either.

Mayerling was worried. His forehead wrinkled into old lady creases. His long red tongue felt dry and his nostrils wobbled nervously. One of the volcanoes was louder than the rest. It spat splatters of thick, blood-red stickiness all around it. The lava in its crater heaved. It reared up and down like waves in a stormy sea. Kree and Skraw were bright-eyed because they were brave volcano-surfers. They were going to ride those hot, surging, towering waves.

"Come on," they said, and with their wings tucked back for maximum speed they dived.

Mayerling didn't like the look of that volcano. He hadn't actually seen any teeth and he wasn't flying close enough to smell its breath. But he thought it looked mean. He glanced around for flowers to pick but there were none, probably because the earth around the volcanoes was shivery with heat. It was likely to fry the roots and batter the petals.

"HELP!" squealed Kree.

"HELP!" yelped Skraw.

Mayerling looked around to see a long, steaming tongue slobbering out of the volcano and licking the air. Unfortunately for Kree and Skraw it was the part of the air where they were flying. The tongue had wrapped itself around the pair of them and their clawed feet were trying in vain to kick free. Inside the tongue their wings were clamped and could not even flutter.

"Oh, puddles!" said Mayerling. This was a rude word among dragons.

"HELP!" cried Kree and Skraw, helplessly.

"Oh, sea!" said Mayerling. This was even ruder because a dragon that fell into the sea might never breathe fire again.

He supposed he would have to do something. But what? It was a nuisance. Flowers were so much less trouble. It was just like his brothers to choose the nastiest, greediest volcano with the longest, reddest tongue. But they were looking so frightened he felt sorry.

"Enough of that!" he muttered, and flew off.

His brothers were not impressed. They thought he was too scared or too lazy to rescue them. The tongue was twisting in the air like a monster's head. Any minute now it could take them back with it into the mouth of the crater and down into its deep, dark stomach.

But Mayerling was flying as fast as his small wings would allow. He was soon home, and flying above the pan of spiced slug chilli that his mother had left on the fire. Maya landed with his claws on the handle and tugged. The pan was very large, very heavy and impossible to budge. It was rather like a human child trying to lift a bath tub with his father in it. Mayerling just couldn't manage however hard he sucked in his dragon cheeks and dragon chest. But when Oops, the kindest ongalong of all, called by to say hullo, it lifted the handle with its dangly nose and lolloped over to the volcano just in time.

Kree and Skraw were hovering just above the bubbling red lava. They were dangling so close that their claws were conducting the heat and burning their crisping toes.

"Oh, ponds," said Mayerling, but he need not have worried, because the ongalong stood up on all five tiptoes and poured the panful of chilli straight down into the crater.

There was a gurgle of pleasure, a gulp and a belch. Lava swirled and whirled like bathwater about to go down the plughole. With a spitting, bursting splatter the two little dragons were flicked up into the air. The tongue had juicier things to wrap around now and the stomach in the crater had tastier things to swallow. Kree and Skraw landed with a bump and slid away on a trail of sauce.

"Come on, then," said Mayerling to his brothers, as they flapped about, trying to shake greasy slugs from their wings.

They made a terrible mess as they flew home. Dragons minding their own business found themselves being sprayed from above by greasy slugs. But Oops the ongalong very kindly doused the brothers down with water, which made them scream and whimper and pout. They sat at home and shivered while their clean scales cooled to blue. So Mayerling had to breathe fire first at one and then the other until they recovered. It wore him out.

When Shika came home she had to start cooking all over again. But she thanked the ongalong for its trouble, keeping well away in case it sneezed water from its dangly nose.

"I'm proud of you, Maya!" she said, but if Mayerling expected to be thanked, he was disappointed.

"He spoiled our fun," complained Kree, sniffing.

"That tongue was a wild ride," mumbled Skraw.

"All right," said Maya. "Next time I'll let a live volcano swallow you and spit out your hard bits."

Shika laughed.

"Which bits do you think would be hardest?" she asked.

"Their heads," said Phue, and yawned. "All bone and no brain."

That made Maya wonder about ongalongs. They were so squidgy he wasn't sure they had any hard bits at all. His brothers said they were dopey, but Mayerling thought they were mostly heart. That was why he decided that Oops the ongalong was the best friend anyone could have.

OOPS THE ONGALONG

Oops the ongalong was used to being large and lollopy. And he was used to being ignored. In fact, he was used to being used. He didn't mind a bit, because he loved being helpful if only he could. Ongalongs were as quiet and modest as dragons were showy and boastful. They didn't expect to be thanked or praised.

Ongalongs were not handsome, elegant or cool. Their skin was covered in bumpy swellings, as if they had been bitten all over by a stinger. They were the colour of an orange that is starting to rot on the ground. Their noses, as we know, were long and strong enough to lift pans of hot food. But they never knew quite how to hang without looking silly, and tended to drip and sniffle in a way that was not polite. Their five legs were as thick as tree trunks but it was the middle one under their sagging tummies that was the toughest. If it had to, it could support the whole baggy, saggy, wobbly body, while the other four legs kicked the air for the fun of it. Most ongalongs could spin on the middle leg so that the other four whizzed round in a blurry circle like the helicopter blades in our world. It was their only trick and it made them dizzy.

But it was a trick that Oops the ongalong had never been able to do. Whenever he tried, he just toppled over in an embarrassing heap of legs, and had to use his nose to untangle them. He had a theory that his ears were to blame, because they were the flappiest, saggiest, wobbliest ears for miles. They were so big that you might expect his hearing to be sharp as radar, but it wasn't. Oops the ongalong was so deaf he was always saying, "Sorry?" Except, that is, when he was saying, "Oops".

Of course the dragons ruled the skies and ongalongs couldn't jump far from the squelchy ground. They spent most of their time eating, grazing the bluest grass and saving room for the sweetest flowers for dessert. Some of the flowers liked them so much they stroked their feet as if to say, "Eat me. I don't mind. It would be an honour." That was because ongalongs were so gentle, and always said thank you very politely whenever they bit off a petal, or chewed a leaf, or ripped a bud from its stem. But Oops the ongalong couldn't bring himself to harm the flowers. He waited until their time was almost over. When he saw them wilt and droop and start to turn papery or slimy, he closed his eyes and took a careful bite. "Sorry," he sobbed, with tears splashing from his eyes.

Oops the ongalong only liked one dragon and you know his name. Otherwise he preferred the company of the flowers and their friends the flutterpasts. He let them cover his ugly skin and slide down his dangly nose. He invited them to form soft, shiny chains winding up and around his legs. Mayerling and Oops would often just relax together and let their tiny friends play all over them.

One morning, not long after the volcano incident, the two of them found themselves lazing in a quiet clearing in the middle of the forest. Oops was on the ground and Mayerling was hovering just above him, with bright golden air in between. They kept very still so that the flowers could stretch and weave, and balance and wriggle, and dance all the way from the blue grass up the ongalong's legs. Up and up they wound, decorating his bulgy tummy, and covering his back until it looked like a meadow. Meanwhile the flutterpasts joined their wings together in a glistening web that spun around the ongalong and jangled like bells. On and on the creatures climbed and meshed and patterned themselves, threading light and colour all the way through the golden air to the top of Maya's head. And all the time they played they laughed so quietly that Oops the ongalong couldn't hear a thing.

Oops and Maya would not have relaxed so dreamily if they had known ...

Kree and Skraw had seen the living sculpture of petals and wings because it dazzled them from miles away as the sun bounced off its colours. Their eyes blazed with excitement as they sneaked up, catching the air currents so that the flapping of their wings didn't give them away. Of course Oops the ongalong didn't hear them. And Mayerling had just faded into a snooze. The brothers breathed fire up and down the flowers and flutterpasts, blasting them with a wind of flame. It scorched them dry, until all that was left was a pile of rainbow-coloured powder, soft and delicate and very light indeed.

"Oh, so sorry!" they said together, and flew away laughing.

"Ouch!" said Oops, because his skin was even more mottled now, and not as tough as it looked. It felt as sore as sunburn.

"Grrr!" said Maya, and looked sadly at the powder that used to be flowery and winged. It wasn't fluttering or weaving or dancing any more.

Oops hung his head over the pile, his nose hanging so close that Maya was afraid he would sneeze into it and blow it away. Then one large drip splashed into the pile and moistened it.

"Oops!" he said sadly. "Sorry."

Poor Oops the ongalong turned away and rubbed his button-like black eyes. But Maya noticed the water soaking quickly into the powder. As it darkened, he thought he saw a stirring. A fluttering. A wiggle. A sprouting, budding shoot.

"Squirt!" he cried.

"I said sorry," said Oops sadly, because unlike the other dragons Mayerling had never called him a rude name before and it was a bad time to start.

"No," said Maya, "I mean the verb not the noun. It's a suggestion, an invitation, a solution! Squirt!"

Oops looked and understood. Squirting water was exactly what ongalongs did best. Maya kept well out of range while he sprayed as splashily as he could. As the water fell on the ashy pile, up blossomed all the flowers and out flew all the flutterpasts. And this time their laughter was so loud that even Oops could hear it.

"What a hero!" cried Mayerling, clapping his clinking claws.

"Really?" said Oops. "Surely not."

Oops was not handsome, elegant or cool.

He blushed all over and the swelling lumps smoothed themselves down. Soon his skin was nearly as soft as the bottom of that baby in the bath. In fact it was almost as soft as the bubbles.

Oops was so delighted with just about everything that he found himself spinning on his middle leg for the very first time. The other four whirled in a perfect circle, and right at the centre of it his nose looped round his head. Unfortunately for Mayerling, all the excitement made drips shoot out of the long, dangly nose as he spun. Not that Maya, as we know, was frightened of water. But what dripped out of the ongalong's nose was a little slimier than that. It had more yellow lumps than custard that hasn't been stirred enough.

The flowers and flutterpasts laughed even louder at the sight of the little dragon looping and diving and soaring in the air to duck the drips, yelling "Eugh!" every time one landed with a sizzle on his scales.

"Oy!" he cried, but Oops the ongalong didn't hear a thing.

"OY!" he cried again.

Oops stumbled and landed in a heap of legs. The two of them were too busy laughing to notice Phue. She was flying overhead and she wasn't yawning.

"Hey, Maya!" she called down. "Great aerobatics display! I didn't know you could loop the loop and double dive!"

Mayerling stared up at her, his nostrils wider than ever. His heart beat fast with happiness.

"Wait till I tell your brothers!" she said, and flew away.

"Congratulations!" cried Oops.

And he was so excited that his nose swung back and knocked him down again.

ANYANNA

The flowers were happy creatures. Their lives were short but peaceful. If ever they heard of stress, worry or pressure (mainly from dragons in a hurry) they just tilted their heads and whispered, "Pardon?" or "Excuse me?" or "I'm afraid I don't know what you mean." They only had to burst out of the earth, grow, bud and blossom until their time was over. They had to be beautiful, of course, but that was easy. Flowers were good at that.

They were all different, every single one of them, which was one of the reasons Oops the ongalong loved them so much. Some of them were nervous, and tucked their heads behind their leaves. Others hid behind a rock and leaned their stems out every now and then just to make sure the world was still the same. Oops would lie and wait for the shy ones, and the moment they peeped out he'd try to persuade them to play. He tried very hard not to flatten too many of them with any of his five clumsy feet.

But not all the flowers were quiet and bashful. Some were so excitable that all the ongalongs had to do was tickle them and they would dance and sway and giggle until they had to lie down for a rest. And some were best friends with flutterpasts, and liked to create living works of art together: colourful and scented. In fact a flower called La and a flutterpast called Dong spent so much time together that they became more and more alike. La's leaves became wing-like. Soon they started to flutter and her stem tugged at her roots as she tried to lift off. At the same time Dong began to smell so sweet that bees followed her around like dogs chasing a bone.

But there was one flower who wasn't content with simply being happy. It wasn't enough for her to be one of a crowd. She wanted more, much more, and her name was Anyanna.

Anyanna had always been lovelier than most. She liked the rain even more than other flowers, because rain made puddles and puddles made mirrors. Anyanna loved to look at herself. In fact she didn't just look. She studied. And as she did so, she admired. She loved. Anyanna was her own greatest fan. She was awestruck by her own beauty.

Sometimes Anyanna would snuggle her head under an ongalong's chin, just hoping that it would drink her scent in a swoonish sort of delight and stroke her petals with pleasure.

"Am I beautiful?" she would breathe into the silence. "Am I the loveliest of all?"

The ongalongs never said. Oops never heard a word. But in any case, ongalongs didn't compare flowers. They just loved them, all of them the same.

The dragons didn't notice or care. As far as Kree and Skraw were concerned, the flowers were cleverer than ongalongs but not so easy to tease. They didn't have much taste and were about as exciting as pebbles.

But Anyanna felt hurt every time a daredevil dragon somersaulted overhead or stormed past in a blur of wings and smoke.

"Look at me," she called into the muffling breeze. "Can't you see how lovely I am?"

But the only dragon who ever stopped to play was Mayerling. That didn't count because Mayerling played with all the flowers and all the flutterpasts. It wasn't good enough for Anyanna because Anyanna wanted to be special. A superstar. The best.

Anyanna's life had only just begun. She decided to make the rest of it glorious. She planned her training. She was determined. It was up to her, and she would do what she had to do without any help from anyone. She was Anyanna. And soon everyone, even the fastest, wildest young dragons, would stop their soaring and roaring and looping the loop. They'd clap their claws and beat their tails in awe and admiration. She would make them notice. She would make their dragon eyes bulge.

Anyanna had been growing from her very first day. And of course growing came naturally to flowers, as naturally as wilting and drooping and dying into the earth. But now Anyanna put on a spurt, like a runner on the final lap. She pushed every morning as the sun rose. She stretched every noonday when the heat was fiercest. She reached up every evening as the light grew milky. And every day she grew taller. Every day her flowery heads dangled a little higher in the air. Soon her leaves reached up higher than Mayerling's nostrils – and to prove it, she leaned over and tickled them into a sneeze.

"You're getting above yourself, Anyanna," he told her, ducking away.

"No, Mayerling," she whispered. "I'm getting above you. I'm higher than Maya!"

Maya groaned. Now even the flowers were rhyming with his name.

After two days of pushing and stretching and heaving, Anyanna was stroking Oops the ongalong under his chin.

"Mmmmm," said Oops, twisting his head around with pleasure.

"On and up!" said Anyanna, because she had the clouds in her sights.

None of the flowers talked to her now. They weren't being mean or jealous. They just couldn't see her any more, and their flower whispers couldn't reach her. Her days were growing lonely and strange.

After three days, Anyanna overtook the smallest of the new volcanoes. She was tired now, and her stem felt delicate, like elastic that has been pulled too far and might snap. But she towered above the volcano, and looked down with a shudder at its steaming crater red with lava. She had to tilt her petals away from the heat before she fainted.

"Watch out!" called Skraw, soaring past. "The volcanoes will get you!"

"Not me," she said. "I'm Anyanna."

They didn't hear and they didn't stop.

"What a freak!" said Kree, and Skraw laughed.

After four days, Anyanna was taller than most of the trees. But the trees didn't talk to her. They gave her long hard looks as if to ask what she thought she was playing at. The air was cooler up high and when the wind battered her stem she waved around so much she felt weak and dizzy. Her flower heads were heavy now. And the view from a height gave her vertigo.

Mayerling was very excited to see such a giant flower and clapped his dragon wings. Oops the ongalong was very impressed and flapped his ears together like cymbals. Then he did a mega spin on his middle leg that made Anyanna even wobblier and dizzier.

"That's enough growing now," said Oops when he stopped. "No offence, Anyanna, but your time will soon be up and your petals aren't getting any younger."

In fact her enormous petals were shrivelling a little, curling at the edges and turning as pale as a sick child. But she could not give up now, not until Kree and Skraw had admitted that she was a marvel and a wonder and quite unforgettable. Not until they had stared at her, their eyes as wide as their nostrils, and breathed out a flaming "WOW!"

The flowers that had grown up with Anyanna were ageing too. They wanted to say goodbye and give her a tangle hug before it was too late, but they couldn't reach. Anyanna didn't look down. She had promised herself she would never look down.

"Oh dear," said Mayerling, flying overhead and seeing how weak and tired Anyanna was, and how low her huge flower heads were drooping.

Oops had a plan. He gathered the flutterpasts and asked them to fly up and decorate her stem so that she was beautiful at the end. They didn't really want to.

"She never took any notice of us," they said. "She told us she was more beautiful and more special than we could ever be."

Mayerling found his brothers and asked them to come and play with Anyanna.

"That scrawny weed!" said Skraw.

"She thinks she's the queen and we should all kneel at her stem," said Kree, "but she's an ugly old thing and she doesn't smell as good as she used to."

And they flew away to aerobatics lessons. They had both been picked for the team to play the unicorns. It was up to Oops and Mayerling. No one else wanted to know Anyanna because she hadn't wanted to know them.

Oops waddled up to Anyanna and wrapped his nose around her stem to support it.

"I can manage," she whispered down to him, "I'm Anyanna."

But of course Oops never heard a thing. Mayerling flew around her flower heads, looping the loop and double diving, just to cheer her up and keep her company.

"Go away," she said. "Dragons are ugly. You might be able to do silly tricks but you could never be as beautiful as me."

She didn't mean it really, but she was very, very tired. As Maya spun, one petal floated slowly down to the ground. And then another. And another. Maya and Oops watched and waited. Another petal made its gentle, floaty way to join the rest.

"Look!" said Maya.

On the ground the enormous petals were meeting in an amazing pattern, like one giant flower open to the sun. The next petal landed astray, but Oops lifted it gently into position with his nose. When the last one fell it completed the most perfect work of flowery art that had ever decorated the blue grass.

Anyanna knew her time was almost over. She felt airy and she could no longer see. Below, the flutterpasts crowded round the giant flower. Gasping with delight, they gathered on it, lighting up the ground with their shiny wings. Anyanna did not know. But then, as she drooped, the dazzle of it broke through her darkness like sun through cloud. And she heard the flutter of wings.

"They're clapping me," she told herself. "I'm Anyanna."

A mile up above, Kree and Skraw were dazzled as they flew.

"Hey!" said Kree. "That's amazing!"

"Wow!" said Skraw. "Now that's a flower! Better than that big-headed Anyanna any day!"

All the dragons in the flying team swooped down to admire it, careful not to singe any petals or wings. And as they flew over it they beat their dragon wings and knocked their dragon tails together in a round of applause. They were making so much noise they didn't hear Oops and Maya giving three cheers for Anyanna.

But Anyanna heard. It was the last thing she knew as she melted softly and blissfully into the earth.

NIMMO THE MOBE

The sky was a playground, but not only for dragons. The fairies had left a while ago, but the unicorns were faster and almost as pretty. The land was thumped by ongalongs and stroked by flowers, growled at by metrognomes and skimmed by flutterpasts. But there was also an underground, and for the others it was a mystery. They knew about gligs and wibbets, worms and slugs, because they slithered out every day, only to be chomped or fried or coated in chilli sauce. But the creatures of the land and sky had heard rumours that much deeper down in the earth lived the mobes.

Mobes, however, were easy to forget, because they were hardly ever glimpsed, heard or scented. Mobe sightings were so rare that there were all kinds of mobe stories but not too many facts.

"Mobes are tiny and black," said the teachers at Dragon School, "with teeth that nip and eyes that waggle."

"Mobes are dark blue and blind, but have a wonderful sense of direction," said the teachers at Unicorn School.

"Mobes are stupid! They're not worth talking about at all," snarled the teachers at Metrognome School. "Cross them out and rub them away and serves them right! Hrrrumphh!"

"Mobes are mean and massive," said Oops. "They only pretend to be small."

Ongalongs did not go to school at all and made up their own knowledge.

"And I hear," Oops shuddered, "they eat anything that flies."

Life was much too short for flutterpasts and flowers to worry about mobes. Their chances of meeting one were slim. But sometimes, when a flower was found on the ground, its roots out of the earth or its stem flattened like a felled tree, there was talk. Maybe, just maybe, a mobe had got its fangs into it. (It was ongalongs who said that mobes had fangs, and death rays that shot out of their snouts. And poisonous blood so that nothing could eat them and live.)

The oldest dragons and unicorns said that mobes did surface for air, but only once a year, so they were easy to miss. If they had all poked their hairy snouts out on the same day, it might have caused a stir and drawn a crowd. But it didn't work like that. For one thing, mobes couldn't count or read, so even if they had had a calendar down in the deep darkness it wouldn't have helped very much. Mobes didn't know or care about years. Each mobe just popped up for a gulp of warm air whenever it felt the urge.

A long, concentrated swallow was enough to last a mobe for another year or so. They didn't hang around to explore or socialise. But not all mobes were the same. Not all mobes kept strictly to mobe behaviour. Not all mobes even remembered they were mobes.

Nimmo the Mobe had forgotten his name until he heard it echoing through the underground tunnels where he dug and ate but mostly slept. He didn't answer to his name until it bounced off the earth, collided with his snout and tickled his hairs.

"Ah!" he'd say, and it felt like waking up. "That's me!"

But that wasn't all he'd forgotten, or all he was about to forget. Juicy wibbets and fruity gligs found it easy to trick him because his memory was so bad. He would reach out a paw to snatch a wibbet in the darkness and it would say,

"You don't like wibbets, remember? You spat my brother out earlier and said you preferred a tasty glig any day."

"Oh, did I?" Nimmo would say. "Thanks for telling me."

When he was about to crunch a wriggly glig it would tell him he'd already eaten forty-three that day and that was the absolute limit. Any more was unhealthy. Any more and he would burst his hairy skin.

"Oh, have I? I'm so glad you warned me," Nimmo would say. "I'd forgotten."

It was just as well that some of the scampering things below ground did not have the brain to confuse him. Otherwise Nimmo would never have eaten at all.

He had no memory of pushing up for air, but then he was a very young mobe, so he had never been above ground and there was nothing to forget. The problems started when his year was up. Nimmo was just rooting and snouting around, digging and eating, eating and digging, when he felt very strange. An odd feeling spread in his brain and filled every corner. He knew what he must do. He didn't know what he needed but it was up beyond the darkness and he had to find it.

He had been told about air but he'd forgotten.

Up! Heave. Push. Ram. Out! Wriggle. Squeeze. Oooomph!

Exhausted, Nimmo the mobe felt something light and warm on his hairy snout. It melted all around him. Everything was dazzling and huge. The up-above world reached further than he could see with his squinty eyes or touch with his scrabbly paws.

Ooh!

Something dangly and enormous was eyeing him nervously as it squelched in mud.

"Hullo," said Oops the ongalong. "You must be a mobe. Please don't bite my head off with your fangs."

Nimmo the mobe couldn't even see the ongalong's head. It was much too far away from his snout and scrunched-up eyes. But he didn't say "What head?" because he was too busy wondering "What fangs?" and checking with his little elastic tongue.

"Can I help you?" asked Oops.

"Er," began Nimmo. "Yes. Maybe. I've just come up for..."

But he couldn't remember, so Oops kindly brought him a few possibilities, like custard, a rotten apple and a thistle sandwich. Oops liked all those things and would miss them dreadfully if he lived underground. But Nimmo wrinkled up the end of his snout. Something told him he was not where he should be. Perhaps it was time to go back to ... wherever he had come from. He turned his head to squint down at the hole he had made.

"Don't go," said Oops. "Tell me about being a mobe. I've never been to school."

"Oh," said Nimmo. "Ah. Yes. Being a mobe. That's what I am. I have a feeling I've been a mobe for a while. Let me think now. There must be something."

An old memory burst into Nimmo's head. It was his only memory that wasn't of digging, eating or sleeping, and he didn't have many of those.

"Once I met a fairy," he said. "But it wasn't pretty and it picked its nose. It had a silver gate on its teeth and it was trying to get to the centre of the earth."

"Really?" said Oops. "Wow!"

Nimmo had turned his bottom upwards ready to dive. Push. Down! Heave. Ram. In! Wriggle. Squeeze ... And he had gone.

Oops the ongalong waddled off to find Mayerling and tell him about the mobe. Mayerling was sitting with his legs dangling from a knotty tree. Every now and then he spun around the branch and dived straight down towards the ground, nostrils first. But at the last second, just before the blue grass tickled them, he veered off at ninety degrees and soared up again. He was getting good at it. It had been a while since he had banged his bumpy head and packed his nostrils solid with blue grass.

"Never!" said Mayerling, when he heard about the mobe. "Small and ugly?"

He liked small and ugly things. Mobes sounded fun. But he didn't expect to meet one, the same one, right there and then while Oops was talking.

Down below Nimmo the mobe had a strange sensation, and he didn't remember feeling it before. Up! Push. Heave ...

His snout wriggled free of earth and felt the tickle of blue grass. A big dangly creature looked down on him. A flappy, fizzy flier with two tunnels in its head landed with a burst of smoke that made Nimmo splutter.

"Is it you?" asked Oops, astounded, "or another one?"

"I think it's me," said Nimmo. "I forget my name. Have we met before?"

Oops laughed so much he wobbled.

"It is!" he cried. "You're back!"

"My goodness!" said Nimmo. "That year went quickly."

Oops the ongalong laughed so much his middle leg went into a spin and his nose dripped everywhere.

"It can't be the same mobe," said Mayerling.

"It is! It is!" cried Oops.

Nimmo was squinting at Oops the ongalong, thinking this was the oddest animal he had ever seen. Then he turned to the small one with the deep black holes. If they had been a bit bigger he might have felt the urge to jump in one of them and start digging.

"You're not a fairy, are you?" he asked. "I met one once. It had flying things like you but they weren't scaly. They were light and easy to tear."

"See!" said Oops. "I told you it was him!"

"I am NOT a fairy," said Mayerling, rather insulted. If his brothers heard they would laugh themselves smokeless and he'd never hear the end of it. But just as his nostrils filled with fire the mobe turned up its bottom and was gone. Down! Push. Etcetera.

Oops left Maya to his flying practice and lolloped off to tell Jazzy the unicorn the joke about the forgetful mobe. She was looping the loop in her own way, faster than lightning, close to Volcano Valley. But she swooped down to a skid for Oops.

"No!" she said, once he'd stopped laughing long enough to tell her. "You're kidding!"

Oops was shaking his head wildly, but it stilled very suddenly. His mouth hung open. There, with its hairs quivering, was a snout pushing hard against the red-brown rock.

"No!" said Oops, laughing so much he flopped backwards and banged his nose.

Up! HEAVE! Ouch!

Nimmo the mobe peered around him. His hairs were tingling with the heat. He wasn't sure if he liked it.

53

"Hullo again!" said a snorting ongalong.

"Nice to meet you," said Nimmo politely, thinking that the orangey waddlers were rather muddled creatures. As for the white one that wasn't all white, it was almost as beautiful as ...

"Are you a fairy?" he asked. "I met a rude one once. It had no manners but its wings were the same colours as your coat."

"Don't you remember anything else except that fairy?" asked Oops. He wasn't being rude. He just wondered. "Don't you remember me? Or air? Or light? Think hard. Try!"

"What's air?" asked Nimmo.

"You're breathing it!" cried Oops.

"What's light?"

"You're seeing it!" said Jazzy.

"Who are you?" asked Nimmo. "And come to think of it, can you just remind me? I know I'm not a wibbet. I don't think I'm a glig ..."

"You're a mobe!" they cried together.

"Thank you very much," said Nimmo, overturned himself and disappeared, bottom up, snout down.

"See you soon!" laughed Oops the ongalong.

And so it continued, for a while. It might have continued that way for the whole of the mobe's busy life. But Oops the ongalong decided to help the forgetful mobe to remember. As Jazzy said, if no one did, the place would soon be full of holes. And Kree and Skraw added that everyone would be sick and tired of hearing the story of the fairy.

"Which he obviously dreamed up," said Kree.

"Being even dopier than Oops the ongalong," cried Skraw, "and even more confused!"

They had to give him something so shocking he would always remember he had been up for air. Something so amazing he would never forget it or the gulp that came with it.

Next time he popped up, a few minutes later, the flowers tangled around his snout. They bombarded it with a mixed blend of scent so powerful it would knock fairies out cold.

"Whoah!" said Nimmo.

Minutes later he was back, pushing up another little mountain of earth and telling anyone who would listen that he had once met a ... well, you know the story.

A chain of flutterpasts flew as close as they could around the snout, tickling the hairs. They dazzled the squinty eyes with their shine, while their bell song surrounded his brain.

"Whoah!" said Nimmo.

Soon he emerged again, asked where he was and suddenly remembered something. He explained that he had once had a very odd encounter with a fairy ...

This time Oops the ongalong carried a metrognome by the ears. Metrognomes lived lonely lives deep in the dark green bracken world. They were always grumpy and never helped anyone willingly. This one was kicking, spitting and muttering furiously. Maya, Oops and Jazzy thought it would be quite a shock for any creature that had never had the bad luck to meet a metrognome before.

"You stupid black hairy dope!" snapped the metrognome, its jagged teeth close to the mobe's emerging snout.

"Oh ..." whimpered the mobe.

"We don't want to hear any stories about stupid fairies, all right?" growled the metrognome. Its voice was rough enough to scour a pan of chilli and tear the slugs in half.

"Oh, dear!" sniffed Nimmo. He certainly seemed shocked. "But that's my only story," he whimpered.

Bottom up! Wiggle. Push. He was gone.

The others waited. They had flowers and flutterpasts on look-out duty all around. Would he be back? Or had it worked? Would the mobe remember the air because of the nasty metrognome that had poisoned it with his grumpiness? And because he remembered the air, would he stay below ground for another year?

"No!" said Kree and Skraw. "Metrognomes are too forgettable. We'll give him fire! We'll burn the hairs from his snout! That'll do it."

"We don't want him so scared he'll never come back again!" protested Maya. "He'll need his air in a year's time."

Kree and Skraw chortled under their breath.

"What's air?" laughed Kree, squinting his eyes in a mobe impression.

"What's time?" laughed Skraw, turning his dragon bottom upwards and wiggling it.

Not so far away, a snout poked out between the stubble in the field. Oops the ongalong was on his way home when the flutterpasts' flapping drew him over just in time to look.

Was it? It squinted like him. It wriggled just like him. Or did all mobes look the same?

Wriggle. Heave. And so on.

"Oh, thank goodness! It's only you!" said Nimmo with relief. "I can't stop. I just wanted to give you a bit of advice. You seem dim but quite pleasant yourself. So lose the gnome." Nimmo shuddered as he remembered. "Not nice. Not nice at all."

"You remember me?" asked Oops, feeling honoured.

"Of course. How could I forget? But I really must go back where I belong. Maybe you'll be around when I come back in a year or so."

"I expect so," said Oops.

"Got to go!" said Nimmo, and up went his backside. "Wait till I tell the other mobes my story!"

"Not the one about the fairy ...?" groaned Oops.

"The fairy! Oh, I'd quite forgotten!" cried Nimmo. "No, I mean the one about the ongalong!"

"Oh," said Oops, feeling even more honoured.

"It's a tall story, of course," said Nimmo, starting to turn for the journey down. As he began to scrabble ready to push, ram, wiggle and squeeze, he muttered to himself, "Tall creature, but dozy. Soft as rainy clay! I never thought I'd meet anything that makes the flowers look sharp!"

Perhaps Nimmo had forgotten Oops was still there, listening. Perhaps he hadn't.

"They'll never believe me," said the mobe, bottom up. "They'll think I was dreaming. But I tell you what, it's a story I'll never forget!"

Oops the ongalong sniffed and dripped more than usual as the mobe vanished into the ground.

"I might forget about you, though," he said to himself. "Seeing as I'm so dozy. Nimmo the ... Now let me see." He pretended to concentrate very hard. "Oh, my poor brain! What *are* you again?"

He smiled as he waddled away. He'd never managed a rhyme before, not even one that was an accident. He'd forgotten the mobe already.

The mobes were easily forgotten, because they didn't hang around long enough to make friends.

FEE THE FAIRY

When the fairies left to find a cool new land, it wasn't only the heat that drove them away. They were delicate little creatures who didn't have the energy to put up with boisterous young dragons like Kree and Skraw. Too much noise and speed and far too many practical jokes.

Fairies had most in common with the flowers and flutterpasts, which meant their friends were always dying, so they shed a lot of tears. Because they spoke in a murmur softer than rain on grass, they found it hard to have a good chat with ongalongs who never heard a word they said. So life in the land of volcanoes had too many troubles and not enough joy.

They'd also had quite enough of the metrognomes, thank you very much. Fairies tended to fly away sobbing and shaking when metrognomes growled or scowled at them, and if they cried too much they couldn't see where they were going, and bumped into things that were harder and tougher than they were. Even flowers were harder and tougher than they were.

What happened to them when they left, nobody knew. Nobody, that is, except Nimmo the mobe. He, of course, said he had met one once, although nobody believed his story. But it was true.

Nimmo's story didn't seem to fit the facts about fairies. They were gentle and kind and tried to work good magic that would make people happy. They were so light that a dragon couldn't feel anything if one sat on its tail. Very easy to squash, and much too tiny to bother to eat, they were of course beautiful. But they not only looked perfect. They *were* very nearly perfect. Well, most of them were. It just happened that the fairy Nimmo met was not like that. Not at all.

Fee had been named Fiona, but she didn't like it.

"Me Fee," was the first thing she said as a toddler.

Then she flexed the muscles in her arms and lifted a giant toad high above her head even though it weighed about eleven times as much as she did. The toad would have flattened her if she had dropped it. Luckily she didn't, not until she had brought it down again and it landed on her left foot. Other fairies would have wept and throbbed as it sprang away. Fee just hopped one hop and closed her mouth very tight.

Fee lost a few of her teeth when she tried to bite a hole in a mountain. At the same time she bent her nose out of shape in a way that was not at all attractive. It was as crooked as the roots of a tree, and though her blood was washed away by Oops the ongalong, Fee would never be beautiful again.

She tried to work kind, helpful magic but it always went wrong. After she had accidentally turned a few flutterpasts into bananas and made a couple of lovable flowers into biting beetles, she told Oops she was giving up trying. She was the only fairy Oops could hear because her voice was as loud as a branch breaking off in a storm.

"That's a shame," he said. "I'm sure you can do it if you believe you can. Practise on me. Make me fly."

Fee's magic took the ongalong up, very slowly. Lift and hover. Lift and hover. His legs dangled and his nose dripped badly.

"See!" he cried. "Well done!"

But when he tried to flap he fell very fast and landed hard on some rather sharp rocks. Oops had a swollen bottom after that, and his ears were bruised for weeks. But he was still sorry to see the fairies go when it was time to find a calmer and less dangerous world to decorate.

The whole fairy cloud landed happily in the pale green world next door. It was a fresh start for the fairies and for Fee it was decision time. She had to find new things to do and be. She could never be beautiful or magical. She must be who she was and do what she did best.

Fee was tough. Fee was strong. She was also very curious. She didn't just want to float through life. She wanted to understand it. When she was still very young, but as chunky as a slug that ate bricks for breakfast, she set off.

Fee was going to explore the world that fairies didn't see. Fee was going to find the centre of the earth, and fight anything that tried to stop her. Unless she could eat it instead. She had big boots for her large feet and a kit bag full of tools she'd bent and hammered herself.

The day she met Nimmo the mobe she had already dug down a few metres. But she was not in the best of moods, because underground was not as exciting as she thought. It was just dark and dirty.

She did pick her nose, like Nimmo said, but that was because it was full of mud and ants.

She did have a metal gate on her teeth, because her mum had insisted on a brace being fitted before they left the world of volcanoes, and Maya had melted it into shape.

Of course she had wings, and they were annoying her. They were flimsy and they kept getting stuck in tunnels. So she tied them up with a strip of tree root that she snapped off with her tiny fists.

As for being rude, Fee would have been offended if she had known. In fact she thought Nimmo the mobe was not very polite himself.

"Excuse me," she said. "Is this the way to the centre of the earth?"

Nimmo only stared, because he had never seen anything so scruffy and unappealing. Her dress was torn, her knees were scratched and knobbly and her ears looked red. As for her hair ... well, it was spiky and stuck together with mud. It looked as if it would crack and crumble if he knocked it with his snout.

"Who's asking?" he asked, because this wasn't a wibbet or a glig and he didn't think it would taste very nice but he was feeling quite hungry all the same.

"I'm a fairy," said Fee. "I was hoping for directions."

"I should dig off," said Nimmo. "Up and out. Go away. I'm sure fairies don't belong down here."

Fee was tough.

"Charming," said Fee. "Thanks very much for your help."

She didn't stick out her tongue at him, because her mother had brought her up much too well for that, and because it would get muddy. She turned up her nose, wiped it with the back of a dirty hand because it felt sniffly, and kept digging.

"I hope you're not eating all the fattest gligs," Nimmo called after her, because she looked as if she'd eaten plenty.

"I'll do what it takes to survive," she muttered indignantly. She had sandwiches in the kitbag but they were running out fast. She wondered what mobes would taste like and shuddered at the thought of the hairs.

Fee's journey to the centre of the earth took longer than she planned.

At the end of the first day she thought she was way, way down close to the earth's core until she felt the underground shake at the lollop of an ongalong above. She felt sure it was Oops, her favourite, because he had his own special rhythm. She told herself anyone could make a mistake. This was just a small setback.

On the third day she met a glooble that tried to swallow her in one gulp and only spat her out because she kicked and punched inside its throat like a boxer.

"Hmmmp," she said. "That'll teach him."

By the end of the week she thought she must be close to the earth's core because the digging was harder. She was very sweaty and needed a rain shower rather badly. All around was rock, some of it blue and some of it pink. She found herself in a cave with golden points hanging down from the roof like teeth. Even though her red ears were stuffed with earth and itchy with ants, she thought she heard water rushing.

Fee was excited at the thought of a wild ride down a waterfall or a swim in fast-flowing rapids. In her kitbag she had paddles and armbands too. She grinned so happily that the mud on her face split in two.

But the grin did not last. Behind her in the darkness she heard other sounds, harder and heavier. The ground seemed to be juddering around her, and cracking like the mud on her cheeks. A massive, lurching, rumbling beast was filling the mouth of the cave. Its body was like a giant sack with bones lumping out. Its neck was long and very like a snake. In fact it wound its way down to where Fee was standing and slithered around her heels. She started to jump it like a skipping rope until she remembered she could fly. She dropped off her kitbag, pulled her wings free and lifted off, with the open jaws of the beast snapping around her. Its teeth curled in wave-like mountains. Saliva frothed around them, spraying her. It was the sound she'd heard, but not the shower she'd had in mind.

Up writhed the head on the bendy, twisty neck. Up flew Fee, left and right, like a mad bumble bee. She didn't get much height at first, and couldn't understand why until she remembered her boots. She managed to untie the laces in mid-air (with her teeth) and kicked them off. They landed between the monster's fangs so that its tongue went wild trying to push them out again.

Fee was tired already and her wings were out of practice and thick with mud. She was slowing down.

And then she remembered something else fairies could do. She shot up above the beast's head and landed as lightly as she could between its big, leaf-like ears. It could not see her now. She only hoped that she was light enough. If it could not feel her, it would not know she was there. The head stopped moving. Sitting with her legs crossed, holding her breath, Fee could just see the black, shiny eyes bulging out of its head as it looked around for a missing fairy. She kept very still, but her heart was jumping like a frog.

The beast gave a great sigh of disappointment and its shoulders fell. Fee held on tightly. Then she saw an enormous tear splash to the floor of the cave. It was crying! Was it sorry she would not play, or sorry it could not eat her?

Fee was a trusting fairy but she could not take chances. She clung on to her secret hiding (and riding) place. The beast mooched away deeper into the cave, where it soon cheered up at a sudden squawk. Whatever made the sound was soon crunched and swallowed. It travelled all along the neck to the beast's stomach, which was all very noisy and not very nice.

Fee knew she could not stay on its head for ever. She was starting to wish she had stayed at home and tried to be like her sisters when a crack of light broke through the roof of the cave. She didn't care where it led. She was going there! With a determined lift off she flew up to it, along a narrow tube-like passage that led steeply upwards and out into ...

Sunshine? It felt like it. It was soft and warm and bright, and everything sunshine should be. But how?

As Fee's eyes grew used to the light she saw hot rock shooting out of a distant volcano. But surely ...?

"Hey, Fee!"

It was Mayerling.

"Did you get to the centre of the earth?"

"Not quite," she said, "but it was an adventure."

"Wow!" said Mayerling. "Tell us all about it."

He flew to fetch Oops the ongalong. No fairy had ever been so grateful for a squirting. Then after she had told her story, Fee set off home but promised to visit.

It wasn't the only promise she made, but the other one was to herself.

"Next time," she said, spitting out the last bits of mud from her teeth and hoping they didn't concuss any flutterpasts, "next time I'll find the centre of the earth. Or an undiscovered species. How to make mud into water, or rain into honey. Or maybe I'll fly so high I won't stop until I'm sleeping in clouds."

She speeded up. There was so much to do.

JAZZY THE UNICORN

Jazzy the unicorn had never been completely white. From the day she was born, colours had been edging in. Blue curled up from her left hoof and wound its way up one leg until it blotted in a thistle-shaped blur. Red and orange streaked across her back like a sunset, and above one eye was a small purple circle like a plum. As she grew she developed splashes, as if she had galloped across a Jackson Pollock painting. Or as if she *was* a Jackson Pollock painting.

"I don't understand," said her father, who was so white he would embarrass fresh snow. "Unicorns are white. That's what makes us unicorns."

"Nonsense," said her mother. She pointed out Jazzy's horn, which was a normal, average horn like any other, and her wings, which had plenty of flying power. "She's a unicorn with her own style, that's all."

Oops the ongalong liked to look at her from a distance. If he got too close he felt he needed to lie down afterwards. Jazzy was as fast as a storm wind and just as exhausting. She never simply glided through the sky like a swan on water. She exploded across it like a firework. And as she tore around like a rocket she could be heard many metres below, neighing and snorting for the fun of it.

Jazzy the unicorn had never been completely
white. From the day she was born, colours had
been edging in.

Mayerling didn't try to race or chase her. It would be like chasing a rainbow. One minute she would be there, but the next she disappeared. And she left only a whinny trailing in the air behind her.

Kree and Skraw were very, very jealous of Jazzy. Yes, they thought she was incredible. Their dragon jaws hung open as she charged past them, leaving them staring at her pure white tail as it flowed out behind her. But the fastest thing in the sky should be a dragon, not a unicorn. The dragons had no chance of being champions at anything at all, not while the unicorn team had Jazzy in it. They muttered and pouted, sulked and steamed. It wasn't fair.

"It must be her colour that makes her unbeatable," said Kree.

"We can beat the other unicorns," said Skraw. "Well, sometimes."

So they thought up a plan. Through the night sky they flew, carrying a tin of bright white paint between them. Jazzy was a very deep sleeper, because she used up so much energy every day. She never woke up once while the little dragons used their tails to hold the paintbrushes and stroke away the blue and red, the orange and purple. She never woke up once as they flicked white paint over the splashes. They flew away, grinning.

When she woke up Jazzy felt a little stiff, but soon sprang to speedy life. She was as fast as ever. Unlike dragons, Jazzy loved rain, and when a downpour fell from the skies and all the dragons ran to hide in caves, she exploded around in the thunder and lightning. As she sped through the clouds all the paint was washed away, leaving the blue grass streaked with white. Oops the ongalong, who happened to be below, looked as if snow had fallen all along his nose and back.

"Oops!" he said, dodging much too late.

Kree and Skraw shivered miserably in a cave with Mayerling and Phue, too frightened of the rain to venture out.

"I told you that was a stupid idea," said Skraw.

Phue yawned as if all their ideas were stupid and very boring.

"I'm going out now," said Mayerling, who rather fancied a shower.

"NO!" cried his brothers and sister.

"You're MAD!" said Kree.

"You're CRAZY!" said Skraw.

"I like rain," said Mayerling.

"NO YOU DON'T!" they told him. "Dragons HATE rain. It's a deadly disease!"

Mayerling shrugged and flew out of the cave. Raindrops spilt into his nostrils and trickled down inside him, cool and tingly. He sneezed, but his flames were feeble and smoky. Still, the water felt exciting on his scales.

Jazzy was practising for the aerobatics race. She looked more colourful than ever with a shiny wet coat.

"Hey, Mayerling!" she cried. "Dragons are terrified of rain. Didn't you know? Rain is death to dragons."

Mayerling shrugged his wings.

"I'm still alive," he said, but suddenly he felt a stab of fear pierce him like a thorn inside.

"A death-defying dragon!" said Jazzy. "Cool!"

Mayerling was feeling a little too cool under his scales. He was losing confidence quickly, but he liked Jazzy to think he was brave and daring.

"I'll teach you some moves if you like," she said, "and you can teach your brothers."

Maya liked the sound of that. The moves took a lot of practice, with their nose dives and vertical lift-offs, tailspins and back flips, but he learned them in the end. His nostrils were dripping now, like Oops the ongalong's nose. Lightning crackled over his head and his dragon heart jumped inside him. Jazzy looked worried.

"Are you all right?" she asked.

"Mmmm," sniffed Mayerling. "Bye. And thanks."

By the time he flew back to Kree, Skraw and Phue, and landed in a damp heap in the entrance, his sneezes echoed all through the caves. Phue wrapped her wings around him like a mother hen.

"Come on then, you two!" she told her brothers. "Breathe!"

Kree and Skraw puffed fire at Mayerling, but they kept crying "Oy!" and "Hey!" when he dripped onto their claws. At last thin smoke started to wisp out of his nostrils and Phue snorted flame from her own into his.

"Did you find out Jazzy's secret?" asked Kree, who was tired of breathing on his little brother.

"No," he said. "She's fast because she's fast."

Mayerling sneezed. It was very sudden and very loud, but this time it was also hot. Flames shot out and danced against the walls of the cave. Phue patted him on the back. Kree and Skraw, who saw that the rain had stopped, scuttled to the daylight and lifted off outside. They had to train hard if they were ever going to beat Jazzy without cheating.

Jazzy was named captain of the unicorn team for Race Day. They were practising for the obstacle race in the forest that afternoon. Jazzy wove her way from one end to the other in seconds. The others followed behind her. Watching from above, Kree and Skraw thought the unicorns looked like a stream of vanilla ice cream, melting and flowing through the forest. Dragons were terrified of ice cream.

"We'll never beat that," said Kree.

"Oh, won't we?" said Skraw, and when he laughed, his hiss sizzled.

They had given up training and were spying instead. They followed Jazzy and the other unicorns to the fields where they were practising the relay changeovers. They might be fast in the air, but they had no claws to grasp the baton. They had to use their enormous wings. So the first unicorn (Jazzy) tucked the baton under her wing, then let it drop so that the next unicorn could trap it with its wing. It meant they were flying with one wing, but the dragons had agreed to do the same.

"Will anyone notice if we hold the baton in our claws and use both wings to fly?" asked Kree.

"Yes," said Skraw.

"Oh, puddles," said Kree. "Then we need a new plan."

He grinned, and croaked a flaming laugh. He had thought of one.

The last race was an aerobatics race because it was over the volcanoes. The dragons and the unicorns had to dive and loop and soar and spin to dodge the hot rock the volcanoes hurled at them. Kree and Skraw watched the unicorns race across Volcano Valley. They were all fast, but Jazzy was fastest. She was faster than the hot rock that shot from the craters. She also did tricks in the air that no one else could do. And while some of the other unicorns were hit once or twice, and whinnied in shock at the heat that burned the tips of their pure white hairs, Jazzy scored a clear round. No points deducted. Perfection.

"It's hopeless," said Skraw.

"Oh, I don't know," said Kree, and his giggle was steamy.

When Race Day came all the other dragons and all the other unicorns arrived to support their teams. Most of the ongalongs came too, but they didn't make as much noise. The flowers didn't take much interest. Life was too short. They took things easy as usual. But the flutterpasts were keen to watch, and flew around the rows of spectators, resting now and then on their scaly heads, bony horns or flappy ears.

"We need a referee," said Mayerling.

"No, we don't," said Kree and Skraw.

"Yes, we do," said Jazzy. "Oops!"

"What have you done?" asked Kree, hoping that Jazzy had lost or injured something.

"No, Oops!" said Jazzy. "Oops can referee."

There was a murmur among some of the dragons who thought Oops was too dozy and clumsy and slow, but the unicorns cheered. It was decided. Oops glowed.

"Where are the metrognomes?" he asked.

The metrognomes did the timing because their heads wobbled at exactly one shake a second. They had to be fetched out of the wild, overgrown fields where they lived in the drippy shade of thick, wet bracken. They looked grumpy, but then metrognomes always did. They squinted at the light until their currant-like eyes got used to the brightness of a world that didn't have a thick green roof and thick green walls.

At last they were ready. The first race was through the forest. The metrognomes were lined up, their green faces scowling and their green throats growling. A smiling Skree said the unicorns could go first.

"Go!" said Oops the ongalong. Off went the first unicorn. The metrognomes started to mutter under their breaths as their heads tilted from one side to the other, one tilt a second. The unicorns were saving Jazzy till last.

"Fifty-seven," muttered the metrognomes as the first flyer came back. Its hooves landed in the dust just as the second unicorn lifted off and started to weave its flight through the trees. It was another fast time.

"A hundred and two," spat the metrognomes.

By the time Jazzy took over, the team was looking hard to beat and some of the dragons were finding it even harder to cheer. But Jazzy was the fastest of all. She streamed through the trees like a rainbow ribbon, in and out as smooth as silk. The unicorns' total of one hundred and ninety-one seconds looked unbeatable.

Oops had to nudge the metrognomes with his dangly nose to stop them counting, but their heads kept on swaying. Their yellow teeth were clenched. They weren't getting any happier.

"Dragons!" called Oops the onaglong. "Are you ready?"

"Oh yes!" cried Kree and Skraw.

"Go!" said Oops.

"Wake me when we've lost," said Phue, yawning.

Off went the first dragon. The time was good, but not good enough. Mayerling could see the unicorns were going to win and didn't really care. The second dragon made up a bit of time and everyone clapped whatever wings or ears they could. Kree and Skraw were the last two to go. They had made sure of that.

"Good luck!" called Mayerling.

"Don't need luck," said Kree under his breath as off he flew. Mayerling noticed that Skraw was smiling too. He looked at Oops, the referee, but Oops was having too much fun to be suspicious of anyone.

Because the woods were so thick with tall trees, nobody in the crowd actually watched the flyers through the forests. They just waited for them to reappear at the other end. So Kree knew that if he was clever enough, no one would ever know except Skraw, who followed him. And Skraw would not be telling.

As Kree wove his way through the trees he breathed fire ahead of him. He had eaten mounds of chilli for breakfast and buckets of vindaloo for lunch. His flames were red hot. As he flew he left trees burning down to stumps behind him. Not all of them, of course. That would be rather obvious. Just every third or fourth tree in his path. All that fire breathing slowed him down a little, and his time was not the best. But it was not his time that mattered most. It was Skraw's. Because for Skraw, the forest was not an obstacle race any more. He had to dodge the trees left standing, but in between he just flew straight over the black, smoky stumps in almost no time at all.

"One hundred and ninety-one seconds," muttered the metrognomes as Skraw landed on his scaly bottom in the dust.

"A draw!" cried Oops, who always thought a draw was the nicest, kindest result.

Mayerling looked at his brothers. The way Kree was looking at Skraw wasn't nice or kind at all.

"At least we didn't lose," said Skraw, and Kree was much too out of puff to argue.

Oops the ongalong did notice a smoky smell from the forest, because his dangly nose was very good at detecting smells. But he thought it must have been the smell of Jazzy's wings, because anything that travelled as fast as that might easily catch fire.

The crowd moved excitedly to the fields for the relay race. The unicorns and the dragons set off together this time, and the changeover was almost as important as the flying. Both teams had been practising passing the baton from wing to wing.

"Ready?" Skraw asked Kree, and Kree nodded.

"Good luck, everyone!" cried Oops, and nudged the metrognomes, who had their arms folded grumpily. "Go!"

Kree went first. He was head to head and nostril to nostril with the first unicorn. They were still level at the end of the field where the second flyers waited by the hedge. Dragon Two tucked the baton safely under his wing and headed back towards the crowd, but oh dear! The first unicorn dropped the baton. The second had to use his wing to scoop it up from the long grass, and by the time he managed he was a whole length behind. The second and third unicorns did their best, but as Jazzy waited for the baton it looked as if Skraw would be at the finish before she even took it under her wing.

Jazzy was surprised to see Skraw wait, baton safe, for the third unicorn to arrive with the baton to pass to her. He was giving her a chance. She could not believe her unicorn eyes.

"Oh," murmured the ongalongs in the crowd. "How sporting! Well done, dragons."

The flutterpasts clapped their tiny wings so happily it sounded like a wedding day. But Jazzy did not like the way Skraw was grinning. Just as the third unicorn let the baton drop from its pure white wing, Skraw coughed a loud, spluttery cough, and just for a blink, flame licked the baton in the air. Jazzy reached out a wing to catch it but it was burning hot. As she gasped in shock it fell to the grass. Skraw was off, tearing back down the field with his baton safe under one dragon wing. The ongalongs were groaning. Jazzy had dropped the baton! A terrible changeover! The unicorns could not catch up now!

Jazzy could see the baton steaming in the cooling blue grass but she couldn't reach it with her wing. Head down, and wings tucked behind, she opened her jaws and clamped her teeth round it. She had got it! But Skraw was almost at the finish now and the dragons were already jumping with delight. Off flew Jazzy with her eyes fixed on Skraw's dragon backside. She was catching him with every beat of her right wing as she kept her left wing still by her side so that no one could accuse *her* of cheating.

The hedge was in sight, but Skraw was closer. Any second now and she would be close enough to that dragon backside to bite it. One more wingbeat and she was level with his little wing, flapping in a panic as she started to edge past.

"The unicorns win!" cried Oops the ongalong.

Skraw looked as grumpy as a metrognome even before Kree beat him with his tail.

"She's a chea ..." began Skraw, but he stopped. Jazzy's eyes were on him. Mayerling's eyes were on him. The second unicorn, whose wingtip was still sore, had his eyes firmly on him too. "She's a chea..mpion!" he finished, and flew off in a sulk.

One up to the unicorns and one race to go. Off moved the crowd to Volcano Valley. The ongalongs and metrognomes hitched lifts with the unicorns and dragons. As they arrived the volcanoes were very loud and bubbly. Hot rock already flew through the air.

"No foul-ups this time," muttered Kree to Skraw.

When everything was ready the aerobatics race began.

"Oh dear," said the flutterpasts to each other. "We don't like this race. It's scary."

But the metrognomes were excited. Their currant eyes looked more like prunes now, bulging out of their swaying heads. But oh, dear! One of the dragons threw up his chilli dinner. A horrible mess spread over Skraw's feet.

"Nerves, I expect," said one of the others who was nervous too.

But who would replace him? He had trained so hard.

"Mayerling!" called Jazzy. "You can do it!"

"You have got to be kidding!" groaned Kree and Skraw together.

"Go, Maya!" cried Phue, waking up.

Mayerling breathed in deeply. His heart beat fast. He could do it. He knew he could.

The flyers set off, all of them together, dodging the red hot rocks that shot out from the craters and the showers of lava that scattered like boiling rain. It was a wonderful display of speed, skill and courage. The ongalongs were ready with nets in their dangly noses just in case any of the flyers started to tumble into a seething crater. Oops held his net tight and concentrated hard. He didn't much care which flyers made it across the valley first as long as none of them had a burning bath. Or, worse still, disappeared for ever into the stomach of a live volcano with a greedy appetite. Oops crossed four of his legs for luck and balanced on the middle one.

Mayerling was doing well. He had flown past three volcanoes, looped the loop and double dived. He had also dropped down like a stone only to lift up again at ninety degrees. He'd managed a backflip and knew his points score must be high. More importantly he had not yet been hit by any hot rocks and only Jazzy was ahead of him across Volcano Valley.

He blinked with surprise when he thought he saw an eye pop out of a bubbling crater and wink. He turned and saw Skraw, just behind him, wink back. Great gnashing, snapping teeth rose out of the lava and grabbed a unicorn by the hoof. At once Mayerling swooped and batted at the volcano's throat with his wings, but still the teeth held the unicorn by the leg.

Oops the ongalong reached out his dangly nose and hurled a tangle of flowers into the crater. They tied themselves so tightly around the teeth that they could no longer snap or bite anything. The unicorn broke free. On it flew, while the angry volcano choked and

83

spluttered. When the flowers were finally flung out of the crater they were watered at once by cooling, healing drips from the ongalong's nose.

Some of the dragons and unicorns were out of the race and joining the crowd. The rules said three hits by flying rocks and they were eliminated. Mayerling, Kree and Skraw were still soaring and spinning. So were Jazzy and two unicorns. But thanks to Jazzy's aerobatics, the unicorns were ahead on points.

"Shall we stop now?" suggested Oops.

"If you like," said Mayerling helpfully.

"NO!" cried Kree and Skraw, batting him angrily with their wings. They didn't mean to hit him so hard that he tumbled straight down towards a very mean-looking volcano with very bad breath. Mayerling spun, but this time he didn't mean to. He looped the loop, but it was an accident. He tried to close his nostrils as well as his eyes as the lava spat up at him ...

A wing wrapped around him. A wing that was mostly white but not completely. Jazzy had dived faster than he could fall. She caught him just in time and lifted him high. Back to the crowd she carried him, while everyone cheered. Everyone except Kree and Skraw. Too busy beating each other with their dragon tails to dodge the rock attack, they were both eliminated with sore backsides.

"Unicorns win," said Mayerling weakly as his head stopped spinning. "Thank you very much."

"You're welcome," said Jazzy.

There were more cheers and a tinkle of flutterpasts.

The metrognomes, whose cheeks had grown quite rosy in the excitement, were scowling again. So disappointing! They'd counted on a few flyers being eaten alive. Maybe next year ...

Kree was nursing a burn hole in one wing. Skraw was shaking as well as sore. His little brother Mayerling had been so close to the jaws of the volcano that Skraw's dragon eyes were pricking with guilty tears.

"I'm sorry, Maya," he said. "We didn't mean ..."

"Sorry, Maya," said Kree.

Mayerling felt a rhyme coming on.

"Just 'cos Jazzy's hard to beat

doesn't mean we have to cheat."

His brothers hung their heads low. Oops the ongalong, bounding up to congratulate everybody, didn't hear a thing, of course.

"That was fun," he said. "Very sporting. Well done everyone. Can we eat now? All that exercise has made me very hungry."

So they did. And so did the pair of live volcanoes. Jazzy threw the one that winked some jelly from the party, which it gurgled down in a glug like a draining bath. The one with the very bad breath swallowed up the custard with a loud "Mmmmm". Something told Jazzy they hadn't eaten for days and were feeling a little cheated.

As she flew away she thought she heard a very squelchy sorry, followed by a loud and very rude noise.

Even Oops the ongalong, who was sucking raspberry jelly up through his nose, heard that. He laughed so much the jelly sprayed out again in a red fountain. The flutterpasts scattered. The metrognomes scowled and stamped and shook their green fists.

"OOPS!" cried everyone else.

GRER THE METROGNOME

Metrognomes all had names that sounded grumpy. They enjoyed their grumpiness in a sour and snarling sort of way. Some metrognomes called their wrinkly, scowling babies Vinegar or Lemon, Acid Drop or Turpentine. But other parents thought those names were far too fancy. Grer was an only child and his parents didn't really want a baby metrognome at all. They didn't like babies, even the ugly, pouting, kicking, wailing kind. When he was born they both looked at each other with creased green foreheads and eyebrows meeting like friendly caterpillars. They clenched their yellow teeth and scrunched their flat green noses. Together they muttered, "Grrrrrr." It was the very same noise their baby was making as he kicked and punched his first air. So that was the name they gave him. (Perhaps it was just as well that it was already chosen before his parents changed his first nappy. Otherwise his name might have been Phwoorr!)

As Grer grew his mum and dad should have been proud of him. He was the grumpiest baby for miles. He was always making tight, bad-tempered fists and digging his spiky fingernails into his palms with a throaty "Ouch!" and a toothy "Aaaaaagh!" He kicked at things and growled when he stubbed his toes on them. He threw things and stamped when he broke them. And when he started to speak his first word was, "Rubbish!"

finished off with a good long spit. But even when he muttered, "Absolutely ridiculous!" under his breath before he was two, his parents only huffed.

Grer was bottom of the class in metrognome school. He thought everything and everyone was stupid. When he made a mistake he screwed up his paper until it was small enough to choke a toad (which he proved at playtimes, until the toads learned their lesson and kept away from the school). But still his parents were not proud, even when his teacher said Grer was the most bad-tempered pupil he had ever had to teach. In fact they called the teacher an idiot and stomped off, dragging Grer tightly by the wrists between them.

When his parents talked to him Grer did not listen.

"Blah blah blah!" he said, swaying his metrognome head and sticking his green fingers in his pointed ears.

No one liked Grer. No one came to play. The little metrognomes scowled when they heard his name and stuck out their tongues when they saw him coming. Only Oops the ongalong ever visited. That was because Oops was too deaf to hear when Grer called him a "stupid great lolloping loser" or a "drippy-nosed dope". Oops felt sorry for Grer because Grer didn't seem to have much fun. He didn't know that Grer was having his own kind of miserable fun all the time.

One day Oops poked around in the bracken until he found Grer sitting in the damp green darkness with his arms folded and his mouth tight. Unfortunately, before he could even say hullo, he dripped on Grer's beard. Instead of being grateful, because it needed a wash, Grer growled. Then he bit the end of the ongalong's nose until it throbbed.

"Oops!" he muttered under his metrognome breath, and Oops the ongalong forgave him because he thought he was sorry.

"Never mind," he said kindly, and picked Grer up with his nose to take him away from the ferns and give him a ride.

Most of the young metrognomes stopped huffing and puffing and spitting and growling if onaglongs gave them a ride on their lolloping backs. They just held on tight, because they didn't dare look up or down at a world that wasn't damp and green and had no roof. And instead of "Grrr" and "Nyar!" and "Hmmmph" all they muttered was "Ooh er ..."

Not Grer. He dug his feet hard into the ongalong's sides and beat his fists on the ongalong's back. So of course he fell off into a patch of thistles. That made him grumpier than ever.

"Poor you!" said Oops, rescuing him with his dangly nose. Unfortunately, the little metrognome found himself tumbling along the nose, bumping around inside it until Oops (very understandably) sneezed him out. This time he landed in a muddy puddle.

"Grrrrr!" growled Grer, spitting mud. He looked as if he was chocolate-coated. "If you say Oops, I'll knot your nose!"

Oops said it. But Grer was much too small to knot anything except baby frogs' legs, and luckily for the frogs they jumped much too fast for him to succeed. They'd been warned by the toads. He knotted blue grass instead, but that was no fun at all because the grass didn't mind one bit.

Oops gave up in the end and played with the flowers instead.

"Grer bites our heads off if we say hullo," they said. "His teeth are sharp and he doesn't wait until our time is over."

Mayerling had no time for Grer.

"He's so sour a mean volcano would spit him out whole."

Jazzy said the world was much too beautiful to bother with metrognomes who had no manners. She just pretended Grer wasn't there, which was easy enough because most of the time he was hidden away in his ferny world. Most metrognomes crept out for a while each day, but not Grer. People wondered what he did in there, under his green roof.

But they never guessed. Even the other metrognomes didn't know. Since his parents didn't like him, and he didn't like them, he'd moved out long ago. Grer was all alone in his damp, earthy secret world. Or that's what everyone thought ...

Early every morning, when Grer woke with a frown on his face, and the light was too thin to break in to his bracken world, he made sure no other metrognomes were peeking. Then he started to scrape away the earth, muttering at the way it clogged his fingernails. It always took a lot of scraping because every night he buried his secret deep. Then he lifted out the little prison he had woven out of bracken strips knotted tightly together. He opened the lid he had fastened down with a heavy stone. Now he could inspect the contents.

"Stupid collection," he muttered under his breath, but it was all he had.

Most days something had died in there. Then he would eat it, and grumble about the taste. Flutterpasts would try to escape, but he'd have a hand ready to snatch and catch and squash. Flowers didn't live long in his bracken box and soon got slimy, which made them slithery down his throat. Some things ate each other, which made him very cross indeed. The slugs were easiest because they never made a run for it. They didn't seem to mind when he picked them up to play. They didn't seem to care when he called them "disgusting slobs". And when their time was over they gave him a rest from muttering and growling because they took so much chewing.

But not everything in his collection was alive. He had found a hair from Jazzy the unicorn's tail floating in a puddle, dried it and curled it into a bow. It made him feel special like her.

Grer went collecting by night. He wanted a baby dragon for his collection but he would have to seal its mouth to stop it breathing fire. Every time he got near a sleeping baby in a dragon cot it would breathe over him and burn his metrognome nose or metrognome fingers. Grer didn't like dragons. They had far too much fun. Well, one day ... A dragon in his collection, powerless and cold! That would make his parents proud of him, wouldn't it?

Of course, if the dragon parents had known what Grer was planning, they would have laughed.

No one liked Grer the metrognome.

Metrognomes were such feeble, pathetic things. Dragons would eat them for breakfast if they didn't taste so bitter and their beards weren't so grizzled and lumpy.

Grer knew he would never catch anything fatter than a slug or faster than a flutterpast.

"Stupid loser," he muttered to himself at night, just before he closed his currant eyes.

One morning when he went to inspect his prisoners he found they had gone, every one of them. There was a hole in the side of his bracken cage and no sign of any of his playmates anywhere.

"Stupid cage!" he muttered. "Stupid idea!"

He looked at the pile of earth he had scooped up to dig out his collection. It was soft and damp and stuck together in chunks. Grer started to shape it in his green metrognome hands. It was easy. Earth was so stupid. It didn't try to fly away or jump out of his hands. He could do whatever he wanted with it.

Grer made a creature with a fat body and patted it on the head.

"You're my friend," he said, "you stupid brainless lump of dirt!"

He laughed and made another one.

An hour later, Grer had to admit that he had never had so much fun in his life. In fact he hadn't believed in fun, not the harmless kind. But now he had a problem. He had made so many creatures of all shapes and sizes that his little ferny patch was getting overcrowded. What could he do?

It took him a while to think of it because it wasn't the kind of thought metrognomes usually had. But it struck him like the sudden light that came with flattened bracken. He could give them away so other people could play with them too.

Of course many were suspicious at first. They liked the earthy creatures. They were wacky and charming and almost alive. But were they just a mean trick in disguise? Would they leak something nasty or explode with a bang, stain the skin or give off a disgusting smell? Oops the ongalong said he'd like three please, and spread the word that the toys were just as nice as they seemed. Soon there was a queue at the edge of the bracken. And before long Kree and Skraw had joined it, because they didn't want to miss out on anything that all the other dragons on the flying team were talking about.

Every toy was completely different with its own personality, whether it had one leg or six or none. But each one had such a sunny smile that simply looking at it before sleep was enough to make sure all dreams were happy.

"Fancy such a miserable grump making something so cheerful," said Jazzy, and asked for one of her own.

The queue for toys soon became so long that Grer started delivering to people's homes. Some of them invited him in to play, and he found that whether they were dragons, unicorns or ongalongs they were not quite as stupid as he'd thought.

And one day, when Mayerling looked at his latest clay character with its lopsided but lovable grin, he opened his dragon jaws wide with shock. He could hardly believe his dragon eyes.

"Hey, Grer!" he cried. "It looks like you."

Grer opened his mouth to mutter something rude like "Liar, liar, nose on fire," but instead he just huffed and scowled.

"Oh," said Mayerling, as the green face creased and the eyes squished to currants. "Perhaps not."

"Huh," muttered Grer, as Maya took off.

As soon as he was all alone again in the darkness of the deep green world, he leaned in to the stiff earth toy with its crooked smile, puckered up its wrinkled lips and kissed its cheek.

"Yuk!" he grimaced, and spat.

THE DAY OF THE FLUTTERPASTS

Flutterpasts only lived for a day but it was the best day of their lives! That was the only joke the flutterpasts ever told, but it made them laugh, and as we know, flutterpast laughter was quite a sound. It was sweeter, lighter and floatier than bells, the kind that always celebrated and never mourned.

Considering they only had a day to get to know anyone, they had plenty of friends. Nobody could dislike a flutterpast. They were so bright and beautiful they might have been full of sunshine.

There were only a few flutterpast names and every day there were hundreds of new Dings, Dongs and Dangs. Kree and Skraw were always hoping to meet one called Dung, but flutterpasts stuck to their one and only joke because that one was a little rude for such airy creatures. But there were plenty of Dinglings, and Jingles.

As Day 5,473 began, a new Ding fluttered free from her case and out into the world of colour. Ding was purple with white zigzags and yellow dots, and like all the other flutterpasts, the only one of her kind. Of all the sounds she heard for the first time, her favourite was of pebbles kissing in water. She was a very romantic flutterpast. When mean metrognomes said pebbles didn't kiss but beat each other up, she paid no attention. She just felt sorry for the metrognomes because they must be mixing with the wrong pebbles.

Dong 5,473 was red with black squiggles and green ticks. He liked to follow ongalongs and try to hide behind their ears. He wanted to swim before he died, preferably in tea. He was a very odd flutterpast and felt quite pleased when mean metrognomes said he was thick as mud, because if he had a tongue, mud was just what he would lick first. He'd tried to dip his wing in some, and scoop it up, but he couldn't quite reach without crash landing.

As for the latest Dang, he was a dreamer, a watcher and thinker. His six wings were so pale they looked like air and his markings were silvery, so he would look his best at night. Except, of course, that flutterpasts only lived for a day.

Dingling was excitable. She didn't so much flutter as shake and zoom and whizz. And she was always hungry for the juice that flowers kept in their petal heads, because she used up so much energy. She was so hungry, in fact, that she almost caused a shortage and more than one kind of crisis.

Ding, Dong, Dang and Dingling all changed from pupa to flutterpast on the same morning and were soon laughing together because they couldn't help themselves. They looked like regular flutterpasts. But they weren't, not quite. In their one day (5,473) they each broke flutterpast records in a way that no one expected.

That was how they became immortal.

From the beginning Jazzy the unicorn could see that the new flutterpasts were special. Especially Dang. As soon as she saw his silver markings, she thought of stars. She told him about moonlight. And she thought how sad it was that Dang would never see the night sky because by the time darkness fell Dang would have fallen too.

"Not if I can help it," thought Dang.

So he saved his flutterpast strength. He rested his wings on leaves and walls and tired old flowers. He cooled himself in peaceful shade. When other flutterpasts asked what he was doing, he said he was waiting for night.

"Who's Night?" they tinkled.

At first the other flutterpasts did exactly what they liked best and flew wherever they wanted to go. They laughed like Christmas bells. Dong found a warm cup of tea left by a unicorn mum too busy to drink it. He sniffed the aroma and skimmed a wing across it in a small ripple. Very excited, he lifted his milky, sugar-sprinkled wingtip. He fluttered it at the metrognome, who rolled his currant eyes and said that didn't count as swimming. It was only stupid skimming. Dong didn't listen. He danced through the sunlight with pride, crying "I did it! I did it!" For the rest of his day he felt like an adventurer – a sweet and slightly sticky hero.

Ding broke a different record and quite a few hearts. No one had ever met such a loving flutterpast. She told all the others how pretty they were and asked what she could do to make them happy. When Oops the ongalong's nose was sore, she stroked her wing along it. Because she heard that Mayerling had a tummy ache after too much chilli for lunch, she persuaded some of her flutterpast friends to come with her and dance gently on his tender scales. She was so kind that everyone except the metrognomes smiled at the sight of her flying in their direction. Every creature, big or small, waved at Ding and hoped she would stop to chat. Each one of them was sad when she flew on, as if the light had all been drained away.

During Ding's only afternoon, Grer broke a favourite toy and almost went back to his old, grumpy self. But when he heard Ding's flutterpast laughter above the bracken he stopped stomping and felt a softness smooth out his creases, even the ones inside. It wasn't just laughter. It was the sound of everyone's birthday. It was a whole series of rainbows spilling down into the damp, earthy world of green-roofed darkness.

"Never mind," said Grer, listening hard. "I'll make a better one. The best ever."

Ding's music soothed the flowers too. They were anxious because they were running out of the juice the flutterpasts sipped. Dingling had drunk most of it, raiding flower heads and racing off without a thought for the next flutterpast. He was cheerful and chatty but he wasn't thinking. He was too busy drinking. And as the day wore on he grew too big for his wings. Swollen and swilling, he became too sluggish to lift off. And if he managed, he couldn't get far before he slumped to the ground again. He was much too full for flying.

Some flutterpasts were starting to complain in a gentle and sorry flutterpast way. They were getting hungry and it wasn't really fair. Dong didn't mind, because Dong preferred tea. Ding didn't mind, because Ding didn't need to find sweetness. She had her own, of a rather different kind. And Dang didn't care, because Dang had her eye on the stars, even though she might never see them except in the brightness of her imagination.

By dragon supper time the flutterpasts were saying goodbye. Dingling was the very first to fall, and the wonder was that he had kept on flying so long. When he fell, it wasn't with a whisper of a landing, but a thud. Others followed, tired now of flying around from one empty flower to another. One after another the flutterpasts came to the end of their one and only day. As for those that were left, the slowness of their wings and the thin paleness of their laughter told them gently that their time had come.

"What a beautiful day," said Dong.

"A sweet day," said Ding.

They were surprised to see Dang, looking more transparent than ever and flying very slowly from one rest to another.

"No stars yet," he said weakly, tilting a wing up to the darkening sky.

"It's been lovely to know you," the others said, fluttering their wings in a last greeting.

By the time Jazzy was ready for sleep, the flutterpasts had gone, fading away with the day. All except one. Something shone in the twilight on a leaf near the top of a tall, silvered tree. He hardly fluttered, but he shone as brightly as the stars that were waking above.

Jazzy flew down and looked closely. She was with the world's oldest flutterpast. Night was blanketing the land and most of its colour was hidden, buried in black. But not Dang. Dang was like a star that had tumbled and settled for all to see. Jazzy held her breath.

"I saw the stars," breathed Dang.

"Never mind seeing the stars," said Jazzy. "You *are* a star!"

But Dang didn't care about himself. Then all of a sudden the stars he loved had gone from the sky and were bright inside his own warm darkness. Jazzy knew, because of the stillness of his wings and the silence of his singing. Jazzy the unicorn left the flutterpast to shine his last, because now shining was all he could do.

Day 5,474 began with a debate. Which flutterpast was the greatest? Which record-breaker would be remembered longest?

Skraw named Dingling.

"Fattest flutterpast in history!" laughed Kree.

"And the greediest!" said Skraw.

"Dong was the only flutterpast in history to swim in tea," smiled their mum, because it was her tea that had been scooped with a wing.

"We've told you before! That isn't swimming! It's stupid old skimming!" protested a group of stamping metrognomes.

"Well, Dong was the oddest, anyway," said Oops, who was fond of anything odd.

"It's between Ding and Dang," said Maya.

"Yes," said Jazzy. "Two very special flutterpasts."

If Phue had not been yawning she might have said, "Ding!" instead of "Dyaaaaaaah". Because Phue thought that Ding had been full of love for everyone. Dang had only been *in* love – with the stars.

"Both special in different ways," said Grer, thinking of all his earthy toys, each one unique.

But it was a new day, and brand new flutterpasts were filling the air. Below ground, gligs and wibbets wriggled and dodged the squinting mobes. Ongalongs waddled and squirted happily. Young flowers grew and old flowers shrank. Grer had toys to make and Jazzy the unicorn had a new colour, too new to have a name, glowing like the moon in the middle of her right ear. Heading for the volcanoes, Kree and Skraw were soon arguing about which of them would finally prove he was daredevil king of the skies. And Mayerling looped the loop, mainly to shake out the worms that had mistaken his nostrils for caves.

A new day! Who knew what it might bring?

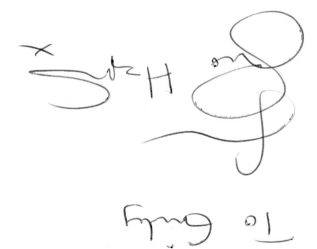

A new year starts with a funeral – but bursts into a very special kind of life as Hattie, James and Beth meet a great-gran they hardly knew.

Winter turns white, and the figure they build in their garden becomes a snowgran with personality and a past.

Whizz is back, and the magic begins!

As the children grow closer by moonlight to the remarkable snowgran, their world starts to change.

Time is on the move, and love doesn't end...

The Snowgran

Like THE SNOWGRAN, Sue Hampton has learned that love is stronger than death. This, her ninth book for Pegasus, is for readers who like their fantasy to seem real as well as magical, and be deep as well as funny.

By the same author

Spirit And Fire (Nightingale Books) 2007
ISBN 9781903491584

Shutdown (Nightingale Books) 2007
ISBN 9781903491591

Voice Of The Aspen (Nightingale Books) 2007
ISBN 9781903491607

Just For One Day (Pegasus) 2008
ISBN 9781903490372

The Lincoln Imp (Pegasus) 2009
ISBN 9781903490389

The Waterhouse Girl (Pegasus) 2009
ISBN 9781903490426

Twinside Out (Pegasus) 2010
ISBN 9781903490457

Traces (Pegasus) 2010
ISBN 9781903490464

The Snowgran and Ongalonging

To Emily Slay, winner of Sue Hampton Mastermind 2010, and a talented young writer. Congratulations.

Sue Hampton

The Snowgran and
Ongalonging

Pegasus

A CIP catalogue record for this title is
available from the British Library

ISBN-978 1903490 471

*Pegasus is an imprint of
Pegasus Elliot MacKenzie Publishers Ltd.*
www.pegasuspublishers.com

First Published in 2010

**Pegasus
Sheraton House Castle Park
Cambridge CB3 0AX England**

Printed & Bound in Great Britain

Chapter One

She wasn't a snowgran at the beginning. To the children, she was more of a mystery.

When she died, soon after a new year began, it was Hattie who understood best. Not just because she was eight, but because her cat had already been run over.

It was different for her brother and sister. James was five and lived for Lego. And Beth was only three and a half and cried. But her tears were because of the pizza, not the death.

When their mum rushed off, calling out from the gate that Beth's favourite pizza was in the freezer, the youngest member of the family bounced with excitement. But their dad didn't think to remove the dough from the plastic circle underneath it. The kitchen smelt bad and the melted white stuff that stretched all over the bottom of the pizza wasn't cheese.

"It's not very helpful," he told a sobbing Beth, "to make a scene about pizza at a time like this."

"A time like what?" asked James.

Their father missed the toast as it shot out onto the floor. He picked it up and examined it for fluff.

"There's a death in the family," he said.

Beth looked round the kitchen.

"Where?"

When Dad said their great grandmother had passed away, it didn't help. She didn't know about the kind of *way* you could *pass* or who you would pass it to. She only knew about passing the ketchup, which she wasn't usually ready to do because it took her ages to squeeze enough for herself.

"We met Great Grandma in the home, remember," said Hattie, "the big old house full of buggies."

The old people had been in wheelchairs really, but it seemed to Hattie that her little sister knew next to nothing. She was surprised Beth could remember anything about the visits, because their great gran had been poorly for ages, too poorly for children. And before that Beth had been too small for anything much at all.

"Not buggies! Wheeechairs," said Beth, which would have made James laugh if he hadn't been worried about the death, and what they were going to eat.

Hattie was remembering a smell of Sunday gravy. Beth was picturing hands that held hers a moment. They'd looked like a bird's.

"Did she have claws?" she asked.

"That's rude," said James. Beth's mouth opened wide in horror so Dad quickly stroked her head.

"She did get very bony," he said, "but she wasn't always like that."

"What was she like?" asked Hattie, because she remembered her great gran calling her treasure instead of sweetheart, and smiling more than she talked.

"I'll let Granny Golden tell you all about her," said Dad, searching the fridge. "Your great gran was her mum."

Beth gave him a hard stare. Was this one of his made-up story jokes? Granny Golden had a suntan and sparkly tops but Beth was sure she couldn't have a mum. She made her own suppers and drove her own car.

Hattie had done a family tree for homework once. The dates told stories, and some of them were sad, too sad for her little sister. She tried to explain, slowly.

"You know Granny Golden is Mum's mum," she said. "So our great gran was Mum's grandma. That's why she's dead. She was really, really old."

"I don't get it," said James, going back to his Lego until some proper food was ready. "It's computated."

"Complicated," Hattie told him, so he could repeat it and get it right, but he wasn't listening. He was tipping out the Lego to find a special piece and it made a lot of noise as it rattled onto the tiles. Dad suggested the living room would be better.

"It's a tip already," he said.

"We're very lucky," said Hattie. "No one else in my class has got a great gran at all." She helped her dad find the Marmite and peanut butter. "Can I go to the funeral? I've never been to a funeral."

But none of them went, because they were too young. Their other grandparents looked after them and when Mum came back home with Granny Golden, Hattie could tell they'd been crying even though they pretended to be cheerful.

And then Granny Golden went back to France and everything became normal again. But Hattie decided to investigate. She found a quilted notebook she had never used and wrote a title on the first page:

MY GREAT GRANDMA

by Hattie Sherwood

Underneath she wrote R.I.P. and thought she must remember to tell James what that meant in case he decided to tear the page.

She drew a cross because Mum said Great Gran had gone to heaven.

Hattie turned the page and arranged coloured blobs in a line down the left hand side, using a different felt tip for each one. Seven bullet points. Now she had to find seven facts about her great grandmother. Otherwise she'd have to turn the spare dots into daisies.

But it didn't take long. She asked Mum, who dug out photos from an old shoe box and then bought a frame to display her favourite.

In the picture her great gran didn't look old at all. She had long, fluffy hair blowing in the breeze and daffodils at her feet, which were bare. The photo was black and white but Hattie could tell that she had colour in her cheeks. Mum said her eyes were very blue, and her toenails were always scarlet which was supposed to be naughty in those days. Hattie couldn't see how toenails could possibly be naughty unless they poked someone in the mouth and that would be hard to do.

Beth liked looking at the photo. Hattie heard James laughing loudly at her. He was pointing, even though Mum had told him not to point, especially when the finger came with a laugh.

Hattie had to admit Beth did look funny. She was scrunching up her face on one side like a drawing that had gone wrong.

"I'm trying to hide one eye," she said, pouting.

It was Dad who understood.

"Are you winking, sweetheart?"

He winked at her and she nodded with her whole body. Then she tried again, but she was looking at the photograph.

"I'm winking back," she said, and scowled at James, who was busy flying a spaceship into a cushion.

Hattie didn't take any notice of that. After all, six fairies lived in Beth's empty egg box. She'd put cotton wool in each hole to make the beds comfy, a sequin or two to make them pretty and a currant in case the fairies got peckish in the night.

But Hattie needed a lot more information for her file. She emailed Granny Golden, who said she'd see what she could dig out. A week later she sent a very well-padded package, labelled *Amelia*. In it was a doll, a very stiff one with legs that were in two sections joined with elastic bands inside. It had a mouth with the red paint almost worn away, which Beth said was too hard to kiss. The eyes were like marbles that slid with a little clunk when Beth tipped her one way and then the other. But most disappointing of all was the doll's hair. It wasn't long or glossy. It was like the bit of carpet where the iron had landed when James knocked it. Amelia's hair was worn and matted and had no shine.

Beth didn't like Amelia at all and when she threw her on the sofa the doll's head tilted back as if it might snap off. But Hattie promised she would take very good care of Amelia, because she was older than Mum and

Dad put together. And because once, when the world was a very different place, her great gran had loved her so much.

Soon the page in the quilted book was full.

• Her name was Mary Ann Speedwell but her nickname was Whizz.

• She lived ninety-three years.

• She married Bill but he was sad after the war. He died soon after they adopted Belle (That's Granny Golden, aka Double G).

• They adopted her because their baby died and they didn't have any more. SEE FAMILY TREE.

• Whizz was a teacher and her class had 50 children.

• She rode a bike and could do the splits and she played hockey at Wembley once.

• Her laugh was very big and loud and she sang when she did the housework to make it more fun.

Around the edge Hattie drew a hockey stick that James said looked like a Christmas stocking. The bike really did look like Dad's glasses, and the vacuum cleaner turned into a big fat L. Hattie kept her Great Gran fact file hidden after that.

She did ask Granny Golden on the phone why nothing came up on Google for Mary Ann.

"She was never a celebrity," said Double G, and Hattie could hear her smiling.

Hattie thought she sounded as if she should have been really famous. She wondered whether she could make her famous now, or did dying mean it was too late?

One day, a few weeks after Whizz had died, Hattie's book went missing. She turned out a huge pile of bits and pieces from under her bed and tipped all her drawers upside down. Then when she was walking past James's room she saw it lying there on his bed next to his teddy. Obviously she hadn't hidden it well enough. Pushing her mouth and her forehead tight, she stomped in to grab it. James had crossed out a word on the first page, as neatly as he could. He'd changed MY to OUR and drawn a heart that he hadn't coloured in very well.

Hattie unfolded her angry arms and decided the fact file was for sharing. That was the day the snow began.

Chapter Two

At first their dad said the snow was feeble. Beth became bouncy with excitement anyway, because she hadn't seen much in her life. She kept running from one room to another to make sure it was snowing out of every window.

"It's landing! It's landing! It is!" she cried.

Hattie wondered what would happen if it didn't land but stayed between the ground and sky. She supposed the air would get rather solid in the end and people would have to go round pushing holes in it just to get to the shops. Hattie knew why snow landed. It was the same reason a ball fell to the ground when you dropped it.

"That's gravity," said Hattie.

"It's snow!" objected Beth. "It's snow, isn't it, Mummy?"

James didn't know about gravity, but he knew about snow and laughed very loudly. Hattie wondered whether he got his laugh from Whizz, but she thought hers must have been nicer. She lifted Beth up on the windowsill.

There she stood in her baggy pyjamas with her fingers knotted under her chin and her eyes rounding as she watched the garden.

The snow, which had been like watery pine needles, was soon changing. The flakes were bigger and whiter now and there seemed to be more of them.

"God's got dandruff!" said James, who scratched his own white flakes for fun.

"Don't talk about God like that," said Hattie, because she was more interested in God now that Whizz had gone to be with Him.

"God doesn't mind jokes," said James, going back to his Lego.

"Aren't you excited?" asked Hattie.

"Yes," said James, "but not yet."

There had been snow when he was four. He had been so excited he'd forgotten how to write his name in Nursery and written Jane by mistake, which had made the teacher laugh. But by playtime the snow had all gone and everything was just cold and wet.

But this time it was different. The snow kept on. Soon the sprinkling on the ground became a coating

and then the coating became what Mum called a blanket. She had to explain that blankets were what people put on beds before duvets were invented, but they weren't as thick.

It was a Saturday so no one had to go anywhere yet. And the snow just kept on falling.

"Look!" cried Beth, climbing back on the windowsill. "Now it's a duvet!"

"No, it's whiter than a duvet," said James, because he had been sick in bed not long ago.

Even Hattie had never seen snow like it. The three children wanted to go outside and play in it. But the snow was wild now and Dad, who stuck his head out of the kitchen door, said the air nearly bit his nose off.

"Wait until it stops," said Mum. "Then it'll be even deeper. It'll be really magical."

Beth stared. She wasn't sure what other tricks snow could do. She couldn't wait to find out. None of them could settle to anything except snow-watching, so Mum suggested that they put aprons on and made snow biscuits with white icing. They were busy beating and spreading and trying not to lick their fingers when Beth pointed out of the window.

The snow had stopped and the garden shone under a sky that grew bluer as they watched.

"YES!" said James, tugging at his apron and fighting it off.

Beth held her arms up to Hattie, but it wasn't easy to free her because she was jumping up and down. Beth was last out of the door because she had to have icing removed from her nose, chin, fingernails and hair. She ran so fast that she fell, face down into the snow.

James laughed. Beth cried, so Dad picked her up, but she wriggled out of his arms. One word said it all, and more than one person said:

"Snowman!"

Dad and James rolled the body and Hattie and Beth built a small lumpy head that made James laugh when they sat it on top. Dad said it looked as if someone had hit it with a frying pan. So he rolled the head around again until it was more of a ball and less of an accident. While Dad patted the join into a fat neck, Beth helped the others smooth all over its tummy and back and chest.

Then came the first magic. It wasn't a witch or a wizard who worked it, but Mum. She did Art for A level when she was at school, and even more than watercolours she liked sculpture. She said the snow was harder to shape than clay, and she warned it would take

a while, so the others had a snowball fight while they waited. Beth found she didn't know whether she was laughing or crying when the snowballs hit her.

Then when Mum had finished, all the others stared.

"She's alive!" said Dad, and put his arm round Mum. He rubbed her frozen fingers in his gloves.

"It's an old lady!" said Beth.

There was something about the face, with the wide mouth and delicate eyebrows lifting cheerfully, that made it look female. All the lines of the nose and curves of the cheeks were carved. No extras. Just a happy expression, pale but shiny.

"She's not right," said James. "She's supposed to have a carrot."

"No," said Beth. "A fat zoomer."

James laughed, and repeated, "Fat zoomer! Fat zoomer!" holding his stomach until Dad had to ask him whether that was strictly necessary.

Beth didn't see the joke.

"Come with me, darling," said Mum, and took her hand. "A satsuma is a very good idea, but I've got a better one."

The others kept snowballing and when Mum came back outside with a bag of bits, she told them not to look.

Beth was smiling now, because she had a very special job and she loved to help, especially when James and Hattie didn't.

"Ready!" said Mum, and the snowballs stopped.

Hattie stared. The snowwoman wasn't at all what she had expected. Not a satsuma in sight, or a clementine either, or a carrot or a single piece of coal.

"Great accessories!" she said. Hattie liked accessories, even the ones in Christmas crackers.

And they were. Mum hadn't used a long woolly scarf but a long necklace threaded with red beads. Bright dangly earrings hooked through the snow where the ears would be. Something with tassels called a poncho spread over the shoulders. And over the head was a gauzy pale grey scarf with silver sparkles and swirls, which tucked around like a neat haircut. Mum was just adding a final touch: bent and twisted pipe-cleaner spectacles that fitted around her nose and into the snow.

Mum stood back then, and Hattie saw that she couldn't take her eyes off the snowwoman. Hattie

thought Mum looked upset, because of the way she smiled. She didn't speak and her eyes were shiny.

"It's just like her!" Dad said.

"Who?" asked James.

"Is it me? Is it me?" cried Beth.

Hattie shook her head at her sister.

"Whizz," she said. "It's like Great Gran."

Dad fetched his camera and they all posed with the snowgran, arms around each other and gently around her. They sent the pictures to GG's phone.

At bedtime Beth was back on the windowsill in her pyjamas, peeking through the curtains at the snowgran. Hattie tried to pick a last snake of icing from her red-blond curls.

"Night night," Beth said to the snowgran, and waved. "Sleep tight, treasure."

Hattie looked up at her little sister's face. Her cheeks were very pink.

"Why did you say that?" she asked when she had helped her down.

Beth crossed to her bed and slid inside.

"That's what she told me," she said, and rolled over for sleep.

But Hattie didn't know, not then. It was much later, when Mum kissed her goodnight and pulled the door ajar behind her that she heard a voice. It wasn't from the doorway. It felt cool and soft as ice cream inside her head.

"You too, treasure."

Hattie smiled as she closed her eyes.

Chapter Three

That night had three episodes. The first and last would have been so boring that all the viewers would have switched over, because for hours and hours the only action was sleep. (When they talked about this afterwards Hattie told James that his snoring might have been quite funny. A highlight.) But in the middle was an episode so exciting that a Hollywood director might have come knocking with a film crew if he or she had known. Only nobody knew. Nobody except the three children and the snowgran herself.

In stories magical nights are always moonlit, and often starlit too. So was this one, but the street lamps on the side of the road were more powerful. Hattie, James and Beth were asleep. They didn't expect to explore the sky, the cold night air or the new snow that had been falling since late evening.

It was Hattie who heard something thud against her window, so softly that it might have been a bird. Except that after the thud came singing, the kind with

words and no beak. As she pulled back the curtains she looked down on the back garden. It was bright and gleaming and as neat as a birthday cake before the party has begun. All the footprints from the day before had been hidden for ever. But where ...?

The snowgran was not where they had built her, near the apple tree in front of the hedge.

Hattie felt a tug on her pyjama trousers. Luckily the small hand was too sleepy to pull anything down. Beth was creased and mussed, but not too dozy to step up on her toy box to see. Neither of them said a word. They only stared because there, dancing like a ballerina, was the missing snowgran. Not missing at all. She was singing as she pointed her snowy toes. Opening the window they heard the words:

"I could have danced all night,

I could have danced all night,

di dum di dum di dee.

I could have danced all night,

I could have danced all night... with a very handsome tree."

At that point the snowgran curtseyed to the apple tree. Beth thought it was a very rude tree not to bow back. The snowgran grinned like a little girl and rolled a snowball which she threw up at them. This time it didn't thud like a bird because Hattie caught it, and threw it back. The snowgran watched it, dodging like a boxer, eyes on the snowball until she threw herself at it like a goalkeeper and held it high like the F.A. Cup.

"What's going on?" asked James, who had stumbled into the girls' room and wanted to see what they were laughing at.

Down below, the snowgran was gathering up the four corners of a huge white sheet of snow. Even though she only held one of them the other three kept floating in the air, like a safety net rippling gently under the window. There was only one thing to do and they did it, one after another. They jumped, down onto the soft snowy sheet and off again in one bounce. The air did not bite their noses off. In fact it was as warm as a handshake. And when the snowgran hugged them, she felt fleshy and cardigan-smooth, even though she was the brightest, whitest, shiniest thing in the whole garden.

Beth's hug came last, while James attacked Hattie with a snowball from behind. As a chase began the

other two didn't see the snowgran lift up her poncho. They didn't see her gently pull out something she'd been keeping inside. It was small and tucked in like a snowy package, but it wriggled underneath. The snowgran smiled and cuddled it. Then she tiptoed up to reach the branches of the rude tree and carefully set the bundle down between them. She patted it and smiled.

"Let's go," she called, and scooped Beth up into a snowy piggy back. Then she grabbed James and Hattie, one hand each, and they ran towards the garage. Except that when they ran, it wasn't heavy, trudging and difficult, a kind of wading. It was skimming. They skimmed the snow as if their feet were wings, light but powerful too.

The sledge their dad had left leaning against the wall was buried in snow. One blow each and it was red again. The snowgran balanced it on one fat snowy finger and spun it like a top until it flew, round and round and upside down all the way onto the roof of the house. There it stopped, right at the very top of the slope, as if it was waiting for them.

Beth hoped the snowgran was going to balance her on one finger and spin her up to the roof like the red sledge. But no! She was climbing. Still up on her snow back, Beth held on tightly as the snowgran shinned up the drainpipe like a monkey, pulling herself up by her

legs while she carried James and Hattie like shopping
bags. They climbed up the sloping roof as if their feet
were sticking to the snow like magnets to metal. And
they sat on the red sledge, with the snowgran at the
back and the other three between her wide snow legs,
held on by fat and stretchy snowy arms.

"Wheee!" she cried.

They were off! Down they sped, down and down,
as if the roof was not a roof at all but the highest ski
slope in the world. On and on, faster and faster, so that
the deep black sky and the creamy custard moon and
the flecks that were stars all danced and tumbled
around them. And the whiteness stretched and curved
and rushed them on as if they would never stop.

Until they landed on the pond. Which didn't crack
into splashes, but grew and spread, and flowed. It
poured like the milk that had flowed through the
kitchen the day Beth dropped the bottles she'd tucked
under her arms. Black and glossy with a silver coating,
the pond snaked out across the garden and through the
hedge into the woods. And chasing it, skating on its
setting surface, was the snowgran, both arms and one
leg in the air. The children followed after her, gliding
too, letting the slippery surface whisk them along. Beth
had perfect balance, even when she spun along on her
bottom instead of her toes. Hattie did a triple salco.

James flung himself onto his tummy like a rugby player scoring a try. He laughed so loudly that Hattie thought the ice would split underneath him. And the snowgran spun like a corkscrew, turning so fast in a sparkly blur that James told her to stop or she'd end up in Australia.

"You are the champions ..." sang the snowgran. She hung snow medals round all three necks and said, "Shhh! Listen!"

James couldn't hear a thing. The night was silent as the carol. Hattie couldn't hear anything either, even though she tried. Beth's mouth opened wide.

"An owl clapped!" she said, and one golden eye winked from the woods.

"Quite right too," said the snowgran. "I should think so!" She laughed her big laugh, and kissed their cheeks. "That's it for now, treasures."

She waved goodbye, and as the children started to walk away Beth saw her reach for the bundle in the tree and lift it down. Hattie turned at the sound of her talking to herself, and saw her pull back the poncho. She lifted the flap of her snowy coat to fit something inside. James was running. But they all looked back to see her melt into the ground, exactly where they had built her.

The breeze blew the children up through the bedroom window and let them drop quietly onto a carpet that felt like cloud.

"Night then," said Beth, and slid into bed smiling.

"Night," said James, and danced across the landing to his own room as if the world was one big Lego factory.

Hattie stood by the window a moment watching the snowgran. She was completely still, stiller than the apple tree with its breeze-bent branches spilling snow.

"See you tomorrow, Whizz," said Hattie.

Hattie brushed a snowflake from her pyjamas. It rested like a silvery brooch on the carpet before it melted like warm breath in cold air.

Hattie climbed into bed.

Chapter Four

In the morning Hattie said nothing about anything. Not because she'd forgotten, or cared more about anything else. She hadn't, and didn't. It was because she was afraid that if she mentioned rude trees, Olympic skating or climbing drainpipes to James, he would laugh very loudly. Like he did when she took a penalty against Dad, missed the ball, hurt her toe and scuffed her shiny new shoes. She could talk to Beth. But she was worried that Beth would only crease her forehead, like she did at squiggles that were meant to be words, but just wouldn't talk to her.

Worst of all was the fear that the snow would be over and the snowgran would be a lump, like sugar changing shape in tea. But the garden bedspread was thicker than ever. Dad went outside with the children because he said this might be the deepest snow of their lives so they'd better make the most of it.

"That's funny," he said. "No snow on the snowgran's head." James laughed.

"What are you laughing at?" asked Dad.

"You said it was funny," said James. Hattie gave him a wondering look but she couldn't tell.

Dad smoothed the scarf on the snowgran's head as if it must be too slippery for the snow to stick. He looked puzzled.

"Snow doesn't stay on things with hearts," said Beth. "Hearts are hot."

Dad smiled, felt his and said, "Ah, yes. Of course."

The next funny thing (even though James didn't laugh at it) was over the fence. Because when Dad went out with a team of helpers and spades and shovels to clear the drive, they saw that the snow on the neighbours' grass was more of a hankie than a double-thick duvet. Both sides.

"Our garden must be colder," said James, with his that's-a-fact voice. "It was probably there in the Ice Age and there are frozen mammoths deep below."

"Next doors have bonfires and barbecues," said Beth.

"Not in January," said Dad.

Even on the hill that looked down on the estate, the whiteness was partly sheep.

"Spooky," said Dad, but Mum was too busy talking on the phone to Double G to take much notice.

"I tell you what else is weird," Dad told the children. "Someone's been riding my bike. I left it in the garage but this morning it was in the garden, without any snow on it. No tyre tracks in the snow, though."

"Weird," said Hattie, and turned on the TV.

Just before it filled with brightness she glimpsed a white image dash across the blank grey screen on Dad's bike, doing wheelies and tipping from snow cliffs.

It was a good day of snowcastles, baked potatoes and cartoons on DVD, although James thought it was unfair when Dad wouldn't let him dig for woolly mammoths. Hattie thought Whizz enjoyed spectating. Often she thought she might catch the snowgran winking or giggling, but Whizz kept a very straight, smooth face all day long. Or she was much too quick to catch out.

At supper time, Beth asked to eat her food on the floor in front of the window, facing the gap she'd made in the curtains. Dad said no at first, but Mum persuaded him, and turned the dimmer switch low so that the reflection of inside didn't stop Beth seeing outside. The red velvet framed the snowgran like a stage waiting for the lights to go up. Beth crossed her legs, sat her plate on top of them and was glad it wasn't spaghetti.

"Is she still there?" teased Dad. "Or has she had enough of the English weather and flown off to Hawaii?"

"Bother!" said Mum. "I didn't give her any wings."

"She doesn't need them," said Beth, with quite a full mouth that earned her a reminder about manners. Mum went to answer the phone. She was expecting a call from her sister, Auntie Im. Hattie was expecting more crying. She'd cry if she had to live with her cousin Clive.

Beth's plate was almost empty when she dropped it on the carpet at the sudden, slobbery sight of Wilbur from four houses up. Wilbur the Wolf was what James called him. Beth stood up. Who said that nasty, mean dog could come in their garden? James heard Beth's

gasp, even though it was a very small one. He stood behind his sister and saw the wolfish dog with its bristly fur snapping at the snowgran as if she needed a good bite. Hattie hurried to see and Dad came over and banged on the window. Wilbur barked back.

"Wilbark, more like!" said Dad. "Wilbark ... at anything that moves. And anything that doesn't."

Wilbur glared back at Dad as if he knew he was being talked about and he didn't like it.

"He's just moody," said Hattie. "He doesn't hurt anyone."

Beth wasn't sure about that when she looked at the teeth poking around the hanging tongue. Poor Whizz was getting a close-up. Suppose the horrid dog decided to find out what a snowgran tasted like ...

Beth pulled on Dad's arm and he got the message.

"I don't like the way he's snapping around the snowgran," said Dad. "Stay indoors. I'm going to have a word with Harvey."

Harvey owned Wilbur and seemed proud of him even though he was always shouting at him. James said Harvey taught Wilbur to bark. As Dad grabbed his coat in the hall, the ugliest dog on the estate yapped around Whizz, tail thumping hard but only hitting air. He eyed her suspiciously. Hattie thought he didn't know what to

do with something he couldn't frighten or chase. Except bark, of course. He was doing plenty of that.

"Give him a kick, Whizz!" yelled James.

"She's not that kind of snowgran!" objected Beth.

James stood back on Beth's greasy plate and had to wipe his dirty foot somewhere so her jeans came in handy. Beth started to cry.

"Shhh!" cried Hattie, mouth open.

Wilbur the dog was nosing very close to the snowgran as if she might have a bacon sandwich hidden under her poncho. Then he lifted one leg.

"NO!" shouted the children together.

The dog froze for a second, like a statue in a fountain. Minus the fountain ... But could any number of children frowning through a window scare a dog like Wilbur or stop him doing what he needed to do?

Maybe not. But one snowgran could. Out shot one chunky white arm, karate style. Out flicked one fat white leg, stabbing the air between her and that other leg, the dirty doggy one lifted right next to her bright shiny body. The same doggy leg that wobbled down in a shiver as Wilbur leapt back, hair on end, whimpering.

The snowgran was bouncing. She had more flicks and kicks than a jive. Wilbur's tail dropped between his

legs. He looked as if he'd shrunk. He turned and ran, and his tail didn't beat any more air. It just hung like wet washing on a line with no wind to make it fly.

"What's going on?" asked Mum, crossing to the window.

Whizz was still as concrete. The children all talked at once. James told Mum what the dog had been about to do.

"No!" she cried.

"But we scared him off with growls," said James.

"I didn't hear you," said Mum.

"Silent growls," said James, and showed her one.

"No wonder he was frightened!" said Mum.

When Dad came back from Harvey's house he said Wilbur had come back whining and Harvey had called him a "great big girl's blouse".

"Is that sexist?" asked Hattie.

"Yes!" said Mum, and told Beth it was too hard to explain just now. That was when she saw the state of Beth's jeans and James's sock. But it was hard to be cross when her three children were showing their father the silent growls that had turned a mean dog into what

Dad called a jibbering wreck. In fact Dad wobbled and whimpered almost as much as Wilbur.

"Was Harvey reasonable?" asked Mum, when the laughing and scrubbing were both over.

"Nice as pie to me. Apologised if the dog was scaring the kids ..."

"Never!" said James, and this time the word became a growl. Not a silent one.

"Never!" bounced Beth.

"He talks to that dog as if it's a rat he can't get rid of," said Dad, tousling her curls. "Poor mutt. No wonder it's so mean."

The three children went to bed early, even before the babysitter came. Not because they were told to but because they volunteered.

"What are you up to?" asked Dad, smart and clean and smelling nice.

"We're tired," said James with a very fake yawn.

But they were much more excited than tired, and of course, none of them could sleep. It wasn't because the babysitter had the TV on very loudly. It was Beth who crept out of bed on tiptoe and climbed up to the

windowsill. Hattie saw her wave, not slowly like the Queen but madly, as if the air was egg white and needed whisking.

Hattie looked between her sister's legs and saw Whizz giving them the thumbs up.

"James!" she hissed across the landing.

Soon they were tumbling into the garden, and for the first time all day they looked at each other with big, no-secrets smiles. And the snowgran's was the biggest of all.

James looked towards the sledge. Beth wondered what might be wrapped inside Whizz's snow coat and whether she would ever get a proper look at it. But the snowgran shook her head.

"No action replays," she said. "Let's be going."

"Where?" asked Hattie.

"A long way back," said Whizz. "That dog reminded me of someone I used to know. But I'll need Amelia, if that's all right with you."

Hattie fetched the doll and the snowgran kissed the hard, faded mouth.

"Poor old thing," she said, and tucked her inside a big, deep snow pocket.

"Are we going back in time?" asked Hattie.

"Oh yes," said Whizz, "but we don't need a Tardis, Jimbo."

James looked disappointed. Then she said all they had to do was close their eyes and breathe the deepest breath they'd ever taken.

"Deeper than the custard your dad tipped on his Christmas pudding," she told them. Her voice changed to a long, frosty whisper. "Deeper than the Atlantic. Deeper than the centre of the earth."

The words stretched out like elastic that never snapped, and everything else stretched with them, and pulled the children along. It pulled them through darkness and light and a kind of soundtrack full of voices and engines and explosions and rain. At the end of the fuzzy clutter of sounds came a clear one that swelled. It was the four times table, chorused with an up and down rhythm that might turn into a yawn if it dared. Thwack! A cane hit a blackboard. A lid shut on a desk carved with names and blotted with inky stains.

A girl with hair like Amelia's stood in a corner. She faced the wall with her head down. Her hands hung down too, and one of them was redder than the other.

Hattie could feel the heat throbbing through it where the cane must have struck. The teacher was pointing it at the snowgran. As she pointed, the snow melted into skin and the silvered scarf into bendy plaits that poked out above her ears. Mary Ann, aka Whizz, had a tunic, a tie round her neck and cuts and bruises on her legs.

"Seven fours are twenty-eight," she said, in a smaller voice, less crackly and with much less whizz.

"At least someone has been paying attention," said the teacher, in a voice that scraped like gravel.

Everyone looked at the girl standing in the corner with her head down. James gave the teacher a silent growl but he didn't think she could see or hear.

In a cloud of chalk dust the classroom swirled away into winter sunshine on a flat schoolyard with nothing to climb. Balls thudded against walls on the other side where the boys played. In the girls' half there were hopscotch squares but most of the crowd gathered around a long skipping rope. The rhyme beat like the rope itself. It got into the children's heads whether they wanted it there or not.

"Mother's in the kitchen,

She's doing her stitchin' ..."

Whizz's turn and she was in, perfect timing, watching the rope, judging the right time to jump. And again, and again...

"Out ... you ... go!"

The girl who didn't know her tables was in next. Not such perfect timing.

"doing her stitch ..."

A tangle of legs and rope and two red cheeks. Two even redder ears, the kind that sprouted out by mistake.

"You're out, Elsie," said someone.

"Again," said someone else. "Dunno why you bother."

Beth could tell the girl was trying not to cry. She stomped off to the wall and crossed her arms at it. The snowgran tapped her on the shoulder and invited her to tea.

"What?" she asked.

"You heard," said Whizz. "Can you come?"

Elsie smiled slowly.

"Yes," she said. "All right."

Then in a warm rush of baking smells, sweet and fruity, spiced and floury, they were lifted on an

embroidered table cloth and dropped in the shade of a tree. Whizz and the sad girl who couldn't skip sat on a rug looking full and sticky. Amelia sat on the snowgran's pink, creased lap. Her lips were perfectly red and her eyes were bright, but it was her hair that took Hattie and Beth by surprise. It was almost glossy. Whizz was brushing it gently and wrapping a red ribbon round it.

"Can I hold her?" asked the girl.

Whizz tied the bow and smoothed Amelia's dress. She handed her over with a smile. Elsie sat her on her knees for a moment. Then she pulled her to her chest, both arms crossed, as if she would never give her up. As if she thought Whizz would pull an angry face and try to snatch her away. As if there would be a fight and plaits would be pulled, harder than carrots.

But Whizz just made a daisy chain for Elsie's wrist.

"No one ever invited me to tea before," said Elsie, licking a glittery sprinkle of leftover sugar from the corner of her mouth.

The grains of sweetness spun through the air like snowflakes. The children were tossed, like Granny Golden's light and airy crêpes, out of one time to another. And the syrup that flowed through the decades set hard into barley sugar that cracked and scattered into a night sky like fireworks. But the taste in their

mouths dried like ash as a church organ echoed. Through the children's heads stumbled slow hymns sung by thin voices. Black umbrellas unfolded over mud around a gravestone.

ELSIE SMITH, it said. 1928 – 1937. Hattie felt Beth's hand take hers as the rain beat them away.

They were back in the snowy garden. The snowgran's plaits had gone and her cheeks were white again.

"Sometimes the people who are hardest to like are the ones who need most love," she said, and licked her fingers.

Hattie looked sideways at James. But Whizz looked sideways at her, and pulled her snow mouth across like a zip on a purse.

"Can we go back to Roman times tomorrow?" asked James.

"How old do you think I am?!" cried the snowgran, and laughed so loudly James had to join in. When she stopped, her tummy settled down after all the wobbling and she neatened up her silvered hair. She shifted herself into position by the apple tree near the hedge, like a Lego man fitting in one click.

Whizz was still again. Without a word the three children waited for the magic. The moon threw a disc

of soft light that trapped them and tipped them around on it like marbles on a tray.

They were back in their beds before Wilbur pushed his way through the hole in the hedge, and asleep before he crouched down with a curving back and glinting eyes.

The babysitter saw nothing but the TV.

So only the snowgran saw Wilbur the Wolf clamp his teeth together and bare them in a drippy yellow snarl just for her.

Chapter Five

James woke first. His cheers woke the others. In other gardens the snow might be gathering its belongings and packing up. But their guest wasn't ready to go, not yet.

But what was that on the ground near the snowgran? In fact it grew out of her legs, and it was shaped like a dome. Something had attached itself in the night! James didn't wait for anyone or anything. He pulled on his coat at the kitchen door, unlocked and stepped into his wellies. It was still so quiet outside that he had a feeling he shouldn't be up.

For a moment everything was still. Then Whizz shifted. It was just a small sidestep but it made a space that wasn't there before. It opened up one side of the snow compartment so that James could see inside. And there, curled up like Beth's hair but scrubby and black, was an animal. A dog that looked like Wilbur the Wolf, except for the soft heat of it. And the quietness. It looked so peaceful that when it stirred, more like a jack in the box than a baby, James leapt too, as if his head was on springs. Out nosed the mean, bristly snout.

Out lolloped the hammy tongue. Out poked the teeth like pirate swords.

The snowgran put a lumpy finger to her mouth and Wilbur's jaws snapped shut. Not a yap. Not a growl, even a silent one. His ears pricked and his tail swung excitedly. Whizz nodded down at James and lifted her snowy eyebrows.

James understood. He just wasn't sure he wanted to. But he raised one hand very slowly and let it pat Wilbur's back, let it carry on into a stroke, and another. There was a noise inside the dog's throat and it stopped James mid-stroke. But it wasn't a threat. It was more like the noise James made when he saw lasagne on the table. His hand got braver, and started to rub and tickle. Wilbur the Wolf rolled onto his back and kicked all his legs in the air like an overturned woodlouse.

That was how the others found James playing with that mean, nasty dog from four doors up. Only Wilbur wasn't mean any more, and didn't bark once, even at Dad.

A sleepy Harvey Grimes was surprised to see the missing dog, bright-eyed and frisky between children on his doorstep.

"He can come to play any time," said Dad. "He's made some friends." He gave Harvey a look that James

had seen a few times. It meant something like *Don't you dare* ... "Take care of him."

So the day started well. But Mum saved the bad news for the end of breakfast. Their cousin Clive was coming to stay.

"Only for two days," she said, seeing their faces, "until term starts."

"Does he have to?" asked Hattie.

"Why is he coming?" asked Beth.

"He's horrible," said James, who used to like his big cousin until he broke up his Lego space station and took every single wheel in the box.

Mum didn't answer. Hattie had heard her talking with Dad about him being difficult and giving her sister, Auntie Im, a hard time. Clive was their only cousin and he didn't like them either. He was eight and skinny, with hair he gelled into a 3D shape.

Granny Golden wouldn't have him in her house in France until he learned some manners. He was banned. Hattie thought Mum should make the same rule. James sulked. Beth talked to her fairies about hiding when her cousin was in the house.

But when the post brought more photos from Double G, the children forgot about Clive for a while.

There was Bill, Whizz's husband, with his arm round Whizz. They looked young but their clothes didn't.

There was a baby. The photo had ribbon stitched all around it, and a knitted bootee hanging by a staple from it. It was all on its own in a brown envelope when Mum pulled it out. She said it wasn't Granny Golden. It was the baby who died. Beth put her thumb inside the bootee but Mum said the fairies would have to manage with the egg box.

There was Bill on a motor bike and Whizz riding along with him in something called a sidecar that joined on to it like the dog dome she'd made for Wilbur.

Then the doorbell rang.

Clive.

He had a new leather jacket and didn't want to take it off. Auntie Im didn't stay very long but before she left she said Clive had been more difficult than usual since the funeral. He didn't seem to want to kiss her goodbye. Hattie wasn't sure he wanted to say hullo, either.

He said the old photos were boring and looked out at the garden while the sisters hugged for ages at the door.

"Why hasn't that snow thing melted?" he asked.

"It's the snowgran," said Beth, and James gave her a look that meant she shouldn't have told.

Looking outside, the children saw that most of the snow had melted while they'd been looking at the photos. But the snowgran looked as good as new.

Clive made a noise that was a kind of Huh! through his nose.

"It doesn't look like her," he said.

"It does!" cried Beth.

"She lost her marbles in the end," said Clive.

"No she didn't," said Hattie.

Beth was giving her cousin a hard look and Hattie knew she didn't understand the marbles any more than the squiggles on a page.

"She didn't," Beth said. "We helped her find them. So there."

"Let's go outside," said Clive, just as Mum came in and said fresh air was a good idea. So the three children found themselves in the garden, trying not to look at Whizz.

"Do you like my new trainers?" asked Clive.

"I like pink ones," said Beth.

"Have you still got that little BMX bike?" Clive asked James, making it sound like *Do you still wear nappies?* James didn't feel like answering, because he liked his old bike.

At that moment, when the three children were wondering a) what they could do with Clive and b) what Clive might do next, Wilbur loped in.

James enjoyed the look of fear on Clive's face. But it didn't last long. As soon as he saw the dog nuzzle up to the others he jeered.

"It's soppy!" he said.

Beth expected Wilbur to snarl at that. She wanted him to. But then she thought he might not understand words in the air any more than she understood words on a page.

Clive rolled a thin sort of snowball from the leftovers and aimed it at Wilbur. The dog leapt in a kind

of twist as if a bee had stung him. He let out a faint moan.

Hattie saw the sharp stone poking through, the stone that Clive had caught up in the snow. She didn't point it out to the others in case James threw it back. But as soon as she'd ruffled Wilbur she gave Clive a glare that told him she knew what he was. In her mind she planned a page at the back of her book: MY COUSIN CLIVE. Seven bullet points. Is a toad. A pig. A wart with hairs on ... She might need more than seven after all.

Hattie sometimes thought Mum could see through her head, especially when she wasn't happy. Maybe Mum guessed some of those bullet points because as she looked out into the garden she suggested a walk.

They all went to the woods, even Wilbur, because Harvey didn't mind staying on his sofa. Wilbur kept away from Clive. But Clive didn't enjoy it. He was worried about his trainers.

"Aaagh! My hair!" he cried when a branch speared it and he had to push it back into shape.

"What does soppy mean?" asked Beth and James's laugh was the loudest yet.

"That wasn't a joke!" protested Beth.

"Yes it was!" cried Hattie and James together.

But Beth wasn't the only one who couldn't see what was funny. Clive snapped off a branch and waved it close to Wilbur's backside. Maybe Wilbur guessed. Maybe he just decided that behind Clive was a better place to be. He stopped, eyed Clive and barked at the branch.

"I'll take that," said Dad, and soon left it quietly behind.

James wondered what happened to a dog that bit a boy who deserved to be bitten. He hoped the judge would be wise.

Wilbur went home after that. Mum cooked dinner even though Clive made it clear he didn't like healthy food. She made it clear she didn't cook any other kind. Hattie and Beth felt sorry for James because Clive was sharing his room. That was where the two boys were when Dad had to go upstairs and explain to Clive about sharing the Lego, and where Hattie found them when Mum sent her to say dinner was ready.

The place was a mess, worse than usual. James had his back to Clive as if he was pretending he wasn't there.

Clive was sitting with something on his lap and a pen in his hand. As soon as he turned with an eyebrow raised and his top lip curled, Hattie knew.

"Give me that," she said. "It's not yours."

Clive didn't try to keep the quilted book about the snowgran. He wanted to give it back. He wanted her to see what he'd done. Hattie took it and ran into her room. She closed the door and opened up the book.

She didn't find it at first. He'd done the bullet points like hers, three of them, and the writing was neat like hers too.

- She was a bossy old bat.

- She had a face like a witch and no teeth.

- At the end she was ...

He had drawn a witch's hat and a bat too. The drawings were good, but horrid. Hattie didn't want to know about the end, even if it wasn't to do with marbles. He knew nothing. Nothing! And she couldn't rub out what he'd done because he'd used felts like her. She found a black one and scribbled it all through until her fist was black too, and sore. The page was ruined even before a drip fell on it.

Mum was calling. Hattie closed the book and wiped her eyes and nose. She could tell Mum knew straight

away from her face, but Hattie didn't say a word. She would never say one word. And she would never ever look at Clive again. She could feel his eyes on her, but she smiled at everybody else, and told Mum the dinner was nice.

Clive was using his fork to stab things.

"I don't like vegetables," he said and pushed his plate away.

James grabbed it and started to scrape the carrots, sprouts and broccoli onto the pile on his own plate. Clive grabbed back.

"Hey!" cried Dad.

"Stop that!" cried Mum.

Everything on Clive's plate rolled or slid or jumped onto the table, the floor or his lap. Including the sauce, which splattered a wide area. Clive stood up as if he could hardly move, bending slowly at the waist. James tried not to laugh but didn't quite manage. Mum went for a cloth, but Clive didn't wait. Without a sorry, he left the room, closing the door very loudly behind him.

The family went on eating without him. The children looked up at the sound of the kitchen door

opening and shutting. Mum said not to look at him prowling around in the garden kicking things.

"He's hard to like, isn't he?" said Beth, remembering. "Maybe he needs more love."

"He needs someone to say no now and then," said Dad.

"Whizz said no to him. She said he couldn't have any cake until he'd apologised," remembered Mum. "He didn't like it but she didn't give in."

Perhaps on the other side of the glass Clive was remembering that too, because he'd started to kick the stupid white thing by the apple tree. Nobody saw at first because they were all ignoring him like Mum said. They didn't see the way the snow head fell to the ground when he pushed it. He picked up the pipe-cleaner glasses and put them on his own nose.

"No!" said Beth, glancing outside and starting to sob.

Maybe Clive knew they were looking now. He poked the head carefully with the tocs of one trainer, as if it was disgusting. Then he took a big swing back as if he was going to kick a penalty and the head was the ball. He stopped suddenly and smiled to himself.

Mum looked shocked. Dad looked angry.

"I hate him!" shouted James.

Hattie stared, as if her breath had frozen in her chest. She wished she could see the snowgran's face, but it was lying on its side and it was more like an accident again.

"That's it!" cried Dad.

His hand made a fist on the table and he rose to his feet. But he didn't rush outside, or bang on the glass. Instead nobody moved. Clive was sitting in the last of the snow and crying.

Hattie jumped up.

"May I leave the table please? James can have my pudding."

Mum nodded. Hattie went outside, picked up the snowgran's head and sat it carefully on the body, which was dented from the kicking but not too badly out of shape. She smoothed the bumps and missing chunks and added the earring that had fallen off. All the time she was mending the snowgran she never once turned round, but she heard Clive sniffing and snuffling. She tried to stay angry and not care how miserable he sounded. She just kept smoothing until at last she turned and found him wiping his nose on his sleeve.

She looked at him. She wanted him to know she was waiting.

"Sorry," he said, took the pipe cleaner glasses off and sat them back on Whizz.

"Good," said Hattie. "Tell the others."

Clive went up to the window and shouted.

"I'm sorry," he said.

James and Beth were feeling better now that Whizz had her head back. James managed a nod.

"I wish I had a snowgran," Clive told Hattie.

"I suppose," said Hattie, "she's your snowgran too."

For the rest of the day Clive was quiet, but James kept a smile tally and by bedtime he'd given them thirteen and a half. He thanked Mum for having him and was quite polite to his own mum on the phone.

Hattie couldn't sleep for a while. She wondered how James was managing with Clive sleeping on his floor. But that wasn't the only reason. She wondered what might happen before morning, and whether the night would be the snowgran's last.

Chapter Six

James thought Clive would never stop talking. He didn't talk about anything interesting, either. No aliens, spaceships, trains, robots, JCBs or dinosaurs, Cybermen or light sabres. Just Clive, really. Being Clive and not being liked and not liking anybody anyway. He didn't know any jokes, so James tried to teach him some, but he didn't really laugh, not like James. After each joke he started talking again. James fell asleep in the end.

He was surprised to find his cousin shaking him awake.

"There's something funny," Clive said.

"It's not a good time for a joke," said James, but he hoped it was a good one.

"No," said Clive. "It's the snowgran. She's moved and she's dancing."

"I know," said James. "She can't help it."

His bedroom looked down on the small front garden which was mainly drive. The car sat there, hoping for a wash, and on it, pirouetting, was the snowgran. She waved up at the boys.

"I think she wants us to go down," said Clive.

"She usually does," said James, and dragged himself out of bed.

Two minutes later they were in the back garden again. The last of the snow had packed solid and silvery so the snowgran led them in an ice dance routine. Some of her moves were hard to copy but Clive was really good and made up some slip-sliding ones of his own.

"Cool, dude," she said, and giggled. "Tiptop. That's what we used to say, long ago."

"Are we going somewhere?" asked Hattie. "Back in time?"

"Somewhere," said the snowgran, "but we'll stay in the present for now."

"Which present?" asked Beth because Santa hadn't brought her a dolls' house and they couldn't fit through the door.

"Where?" asked James when he'd finished laughing.

"I think you mean *Où?*" said Whizz. "We're off to La France! La belle France!"

"On Your Own Star?" asked Beth.

"Eurostar!" cried James, and laughed very loudly indeed.

"Exactement, ma petite," said Whizz. "Who needs a boring old high speed train?"

She squinted up at the sky, and wrinkled her nose as if to settle her pipe-cleaner glasses. She was concentrating hard. James thought he saw a little puff of steam fizz out of each of her snow ears. As she stared at the sky the nearest star seemed to brighten. Hattie thought it looked as if it was growing like Beth's eyes. They stared, following the snowgran's gaze, and as they watched the star drew nearer and nearer, until Whizz reached out and scooped it from above the hedge. She held it out on her snowy palm for them to see.

"Tiptop," said Clive, and the snowgran winked at him.

"Is it hot?" asked James, because all around its outline was a steamy blur that crackled faintly like a dying bonfire.

"Warm as toast, that's all," she said. "Come on. One point each."

"Is it a quiz?" asked Beth, mouth down because James had said once that she didn't know anything about anything.

Whizz explained and they held one starry point each. The snowgran started dancing, as if it was Ring a Ring o' Roses, and the five of them skipped around and around, faster and faster. All the time they circled they held on tightly to the star at the centre. Like a mirror in sunlight it flashed and dazzled. Into the air it scattered beads of silver that hissed as they fell to the snow.

One minute they were dancing so fast that the whiteness seemed to be pouring into everything else like cream onto Christmas pudding. The next moment they were pillowed by dark sky. They felt as if they were tumbling, but safely. And then they landed not on snow but grass. James heard the water rushing over rocks in the river. Hattie saw a furry grey cat that used to be a kitten and still liked being stroked. Beth smelt the air, its flavours and its perfume. Suddenly the darkness that buried the garden was not so thick.

"Granny Golden!" she cried, and ran for the white shuttered house where she had once spent summer.

"I can't go in," said Clive, his face drooping. "I'm banned."

"Ah," said Whizz, "but I'm the singer with the band." She winked, and started singing something in French about l'amour. Hattie knew what that meant. She saw her lift up her poncho and check something under a snow flap.

The white shutters opened of their own accord and showed Granny Golden sitting in an armchair in an old dressing gown. The only thing about her that was shiny was the glass of red wine that gleamed in the twilight. Her face had no make-up and she didn't look golden at all. She turned and looked straight at them, but Hattie wasn't sure that she saw anything. She sat up, listening, and started to join in the song, very quietly, so that her mouth hardly opened.

"Mother," she said, as the song ended, "I've missed you."

The children sat on the floor and played with the grey cat. It seemed very glad to see them. Hattie watched Clive tickle it under its fluffy chin, so that its eyes nearly got lost in the fur and its neck almost disappeared. But Hattie kept an eye on the snowgran too. She had a secretive smile on her face, as if she was planning another surprise.

Then she pulled out a snowy bundle from under her poncho. It had a small fist which reached out into the air and stretched out small fingers.

"It's a snowbaby," said Beth, who thought it was much nicer than Amelia.

"I've been looking after her," said the snowgran. "I didn't get the chance before, not for long." She showed her to Granny Golden. "And you didn't get the chance to see her at all, treasure."

"No," said Granny Golden, and Whizz let her hold the baby who'd died before she was born. "I was jealous," she said. "I think I've been jealous all my life."

"I know, dear," said the snowgran. "But I've always loved you just the same."

They let Beth hold the snowbaby so they could hold each other. They all had a hug then, and Clive had an extra. Not a kiss or a squeeze but a friendly ruffle ... of his hair. Hattie froze like a snowgirl. But Clive had frozen first.

"Ow!" cried Double G. "Is that a brick on your head?"

James laughed. Clive touched his hair and breathed again. Then he laughed, but not very easily. Beth thought he'd improve with more practice.

Granny Golden suddenly looked shinier. She lifted a finger the way Mum did when she was excited.

"Who wants a midnight swim?"

Hattie had forgotten! Because Granny Golden had guests who booked to stay at her house in the summer months, she'd had a pool built in her garden. It had solar panels all around it to catch the sun. Maybe they caught the moon too. It hadn't been finished for long and they'd never swum in it. Not yet.

The water looked lighter than anything else because the pool was white all over. All along the walls around it were tea lights, rows of them, and Granny Golden lit them all. They flickered on the surface and danced around the glass. By the time she lit the last line of candles the older children were in the water with their pyjama bottoms swelling. It wasn't cold at all. At least, not very, not if they kept moving. Beth sat on the edge at the shallow end and let the water stroke her toes. The way she squealed meant she liked it really.

The snowgran was laughing now. She ran to the deep end of the pool and stretched up straight. She

77

pointed her arms like a church spire and bent at the waist. Then she dived. The splash was enormous.

"Mother!" cried Double G, looking up from the final flame. "You can't swim!"

"I can now!" she shouted, as she surfaced with a splash and a gasp.

Then she went to collect a passenger sitting on the edge who looked as if she might like a ride. And when she brought Beth back, a thin young man was sitting dipping his feet in the water. His sleeves were rolled up and his arms were brown. Hattie recognised the wide forehead and the way his hair flopped down across it. But she didn't shout, "Hullo, Bill," because he was busy. So was Whizz. They were busy with each other.

Granny Golden sat and watched on a lounger. In the candlelight she glowed again, while outside the darkness grew deeper and very quiet.

"Hullo, Dad," she said, when he blew her a kiss. He came over to kiss her forehead and told her something quiet. "It's good to see you smile," she said.

Then she screamed, because he tried to pick her up and throw her in the pool.

For someone who had never swum in her whole life, Whizz did a lot of swimming. But Bill was an even

bigger splasher and gave even wilder piggy backs. It was hard to imagine him being sad.

Soon the children were tired and needed feeding, so Whizz helped Granny Golden make crêpes. Hattie went inside to see if she could help, because she liked the tossing part. But there were already two girls in the kitchen, breaking eggs and beating batter. They had short bobbed hair with a bow tied on the top of each head, and matching dresses. When the younger one smiled at her she looked just like Mum. But her big sister Imogen had a longer nose, like Clive's. Hattie realised that this girl was her auntie, before she grew older and sadder. She wanted to tell her that Clive was going to be easier to love. But the girls didn't speak. They just let her help with the beating and the heating until all the crêpes were layered in a neat, round pile.

Whizz gave both the girls a hug, and their matching outlines softened like the butter in the pan. As they disappeared, Whizz caught the shiny bows that danced in the air and slipped them into Hattie's hands.

"One for you and one for Beth."

She took Hattie back to the pool and the two of them held hands and jumped in together, shouting "Geronimo!"

When the pancakes arrived Clive ate more than anyone as they sat by the side of the pool with towels

around them and scented steam wisping through the air.

The snowgran was the only one left in the pool. It wasn't quite enough, not yet. There was still something she'd never tried. She jumped up out of the water like a seal, gave them all a wave and splashed back down again.

Down she plunged, deeper and deeper, like a dolphin, except that the snowbaby was holding her hand. Trying to snatch at her ankles, Bill swam after her, pretending to be a shark. James laughed loudly. Beth watched with her spoon halfway to her mouth. One minute there were colours, and ripples, and shapes that streamed and blurred. The next almost everything had been washed away.

Hattie stopped laughing, and the ball she was throwing sat in the air. Around the pool only the candle flames seemed to move. And in the water everything had disappeared deep down below the surface. Everything except the snowgran, melting away like ice cream. The pool lay still as a different kind of ice. Not a ripple. Not a glimpse of leg. Not a sound, not even laughter. Still the reflections of the candles kept stroking the water. Still the light curled and shivered on warm faces.

No one moved for a very long time. Then Clive brought the poncho and the silvered scarf up to dry. Hattie could just see the earrings lying at the bottom and Double G said she'd fetch them later because they'd look just right with her red satin top.

"Is the magic over?" asked Beth, as Granny Golden wrapped her in a towel.

"I shouldn't think so, poppet," said Double G, "would you?"

"I don't think we'll be going home on Eurostar," said Clive.

James laughed. It seemed such a crazy idea.

"Don't be ridiculous!" he laughed, and Clive laughed too.

But it did feel like time, and the night air outside was reaching in. It wasn't cold exactly, but it felt like fingers, velvet ones, wrapping like ribbon. It drew them outside under the moon. And for a moment they waited, neither wet nor dry, neither cold nor hot, not quite nervous or even excited. Because it felt so ordinary all of a sudden, as if they were parcels to be delivered across the channel. No fuss. Just ready to load.

Then came the sparks, crackling softly, as the star hurtled at them. It flew like a Frisbee, but it was hot

with swelling light. Behind it spilt a trail of ragged, jagged colour like torn fire. A long, thick silence held them so tightly there was no time to say goodbye. But as they were gathered up at last, in a sudden rush of salt spray and seagulls calling, they heard Granny Golden say it for them: "Au revoir."

Like a tug-away kite the words fluttered and flew, one voice on the wind. Or maybe two.

"Bye, treasure," called Beth.

And all around the children the last laugh scattered like moonbeams across the sea.